I0675155

Condo Crazy

Musgrave Landing Mysteries, Volume 3

Yvonne Rediger

Published by Brown Wolf Publishing, 2025.

Also by Yvonne Rediger

Adam Norcross Mysteries
The Wrong Words

Musgrave Landing Mysteries
Death and Cupcakes
Fun With Funerals
Condo Crazy

VIC Shapeshifters
Into the Wood
The Shape of Us
Hell Cat
Trusting the Wolf

Standalone
The Common Touch

Diving In Heart First

Watch for more at blackyvy50.wix.com/yvonnerediger.

The sports car was ten feet from the end of the driveway when the brake lights flashed red to slow the vehicle. A brown Plymouth accelerated up the Coast Road at the same time.

Abruptly, the driver of the brown car turned onto the approach and headed down the drive. The vehicle came to a stop mere inches in front of Lara's bumper and effectively blocked the exit.

Gladys frowned as she watched the bald male. He was the same guy she'd seen only yesterday, Vinny Norquay. He confronted her second-floor neighbour with a shout. "You need to talk to me."

Lara flipped him the bird and honked her horn at him in anger. "Move your stupid car."

Vinny opened his driver-side door.

Gladys exchanged a look with Linda, she too, would be delayed.

Lara looked startled when Vinny got out of his vehicle. The situation also looked like it might get ugly fast.

"CONDO CRAZY IS A FAST-paced mystery. Engaging characters and witty dialogue. I loved it!"

- Joan Havelange, author of The Suspects.

Print ISBN: 978-1-0691866-4-5

eBook ISBN: 978-1-0691866-5-2

First Publication: March 2022

Second Publication: February 2025

Published by Brown Wolf Publishing

Saskatchewan, Canada

Dedication

For my sister, Shelley, and her condo buddy, Jenn.
Also thank you to all my beta readers.

Chapter One

Arlie Birch squinted a glare at the Monday morning ferry. It wasn't what he saw through the café window which made him frown. It was the persistence of a bad feeling. Trouble was coming, he could feel it.

He sucked air between his teeth, a bit disturbed by the odd sensation. Only once before in his life had he experienced anything like this. Not since his Sara had sat him down to give him the bad news about her health. Arlie refolded the white cleaning cloth and pushed that terrible memory away. Tables needed wiping. Still, he hesitated caught up in the moment.

Distantly, he registered car and truck engines starting up. The noise came from vehicles set to depart Musgrave Landing. All with other cars and trucks on board the ferry with the small village as their destination.

He blinked coming back to himself. Resolutely, he lifted his chin to watch the vessel slide neatly into its berth at the edge of the pier. This was the signal for the crew to begin the process of lowering the ramp. The men and women moved about efficiently as they completed their tasks.

Lined up on the road, numerous local vehicles waited for transport across the Samsum Narrows to the bigger Island.

Some were villagers on their way to work and had just been the café's customers. Hopefully, those arriving would be customers too.

At seven in the morning, the June sun was well up. They were closing in on the longest day of the year. The warmth of the sun on the side of his face helped lift his mood.

Still, Arlie couldn't shake the odd feeling, but it had receded a bit. He scanned the early arrivals from the north window of Jane's Eats and Treats. He looked for some sign to explain his premonition but saw nothing out of the ordinary. He watched the village-bound vehicles disembark from the Musgrave Landing ferry. One-by-one the traffic, mostly delivery trucks, drove either uphill to High Street, or turned left to take Coast Road. "You're a crazy fool." He berated himself. "You're getting paranoid."

With the café deserted, there was no one to hear him mutter out loud. Well, save for him and Jane. There was only the low mumble of the local radio station in the background, and it easily blotted out his remarks. Even if Jane heard him, she'd ignore it. She was good that way.

Arlie got busy spraying and wiping down the tables recently vacated. It was easier to shrug off the strange feeling if he stayed busy. Coffee cups, breakfast plates, and cutlery quickly went into the grey dirty dishes bin.

After the tables were clean, he turned to the coffee station to clear up the morning mess. He wiped down the counter and then he crossed the room and entered the kitchen.

At his age, Arlie never thought he'd be working as a barista in a café, but it beat the hell out of boredom at home. Everyone needed a reason to get up in the morning, especially if you were a widower with a grown, married son.

After Sara had passed away, Arlie had briefly tried to get a job on the bigger island in his old profession as a mechanical engineer and was met with dismal failure. Things changed quickly in the job sector. He knew age was a deterrent, so too his level of professional certifications which could command a top wage. Not that he wanted that stress again, or the commute. He was over qualified for everything else. None of it mattered now.

He opened the empty commercial dishwasher and began to load the machine from long practice. It still surprised him to admit he liked this job. He enjoyed talking to the customers, hearing their news. Who needed stress anyway? His boss was a lovely person, and he'd thought that even before she'd married his son, Jack. Right from the beginning Jane had treated him with respect and valued his opinion. He would make sure he emulated that when they found a young person to help out over the summer.

Arlie glanced over at his daughter-in-law. She was busy working by the stove top finishing up the lunchtime soup special. He sniffed appreciably, chicken noodle with fresh parsley, always popular, even in early summer. "Smells good," he allowed.

Jane flashed him a smile. "Thanks."

He returned to the café proper to get the next load of dishes when a flash of red caught his attention. He grunted when he saw the sports car. It turned right, off Coast Road and then took a hard left. He already knew Lara Finkle was behind the steering wheel of the flash car.

Without signaling, she cut across the ferry lane, and narrowly avoided colliding with a navy-blue plumbing van exiting the ferry. The driver of the van stood on the brakes and Lara slipped by unscathed.

Arlie sucked air through his teeth. "Stupid stunt," Arlie muttered under his breath.

Heith's Plumbing was stenciled in white letters on the side of the box-shaped vehicle. He waited to see if the driver would get out and give Lara a piece of his mind. After a moment's pause, the van's brake light flashed off and the van continued along the road to signal and turn left on the Coast Road.

He grunted again. "He probably didn't think that silly woman was worth it his time."

Ironically, Lara was now hung up between the departing lane of traffic and the parking lot. She required a ticket if she wanted to board the ferry and had to park to get one.

This made Arlie grin.

The residents were not letting Lara cut through their line. They all knew who she was and all about her disreputable past.

Arlie snorted a laugh as he took up the dirty dishes tub. He went back to the kitchen to finish loading the dishwasher. It was about time karma caught up with that woman.

When he returned, the ferry traffic had cleared. Arlie shifted his attention to the east window; movement outside had caught his eye. This window overlooked the small parking lot which belonged to the café. The deceased mayor's mistress abruptly swung her scarlet-red convertible into the small lot breaking the twenty kilometer an hour posted speed restriction by a considerable margin. Taillights glared brightly as she hit the brakes and came to a halt.

"Great. Just great." Arlie had no time for people like Lara Finkle. The woman was a nuisance. He had hoped she was getting straight onto the ferry.

The fabric top on the car was down, and Lara's blonde mane looked a tangled mess. By the tight expression on her face, she was in a nasty mood. Lara wasn't a pleasant person at the best of times, but she usually avoided the café. Probably she had bad memories from this place. She had been questioned by the cops in the back room as a suspect in her boyfriend's murder.

Why Lara Finkle decided to curse them with her presence today was anybody's guess.

Arlie compressed his lips into a flat line. Customers were customers. He resigned himself to the fact he would have to deal with whatever was to come. He would be civil, even to those vain female senior citizens who dressed forty years younger than their true age. He would not hurt Jane's business reputation, not for the world. No running his mouth even if some people had more nerve than a toothache. He hoped the self-talk would stick but wouldn't bet on it.

Behind the counter, he retrieved the refilled coffee dispensers and walked them across to the front of the café.

Just then, another vehicle appeared at the top of the hill, the current mayor's grey minivan. This vehicle rolled into the lot as well. The second vehicle parked next to the red car, possibly a bit too close.

Arlie hardly gave the mayor a glance as he placed the medium-blend coffee air-pot between the other two coffee dispensers on the back counter by the door. Usually, he liked to watch the comings and goings. He was fascinated with people, curious about each of them, and their business. Snoopy actually, if he were truthful. Anyway, he wasn't a gossip. Not at all.

He noticed Lara Finkle fussing as she looked into her vanity mirror. She was trying to fix her hair. Irritably, she slapped the cover closed and flung open her driver's side door. As she tried to emerge from her car, her wide door would not open all the way. The van impeded its path. Lara's jaw flexed as she gritted her teeth and slowly edged her way out of the car.

Lara turned a look of distaste on the late model van. Then she dismissed it as she turned away to grab a tan leather handbag which sat on the passenger seat. The strap got caught on the emergency brake handle and refused to obey Lara.

Arlie paused, eyebrows raised, watching Lara haul on the bag. If she'd only walk around to the other side, she wouldn't have this problem. He could see she was more than merely out of sorts. Not only was her hair messed up, her beige suit was creased and rumpled. The black stuff, what was it called? Women put around their eyes, mascara, yeah, it was smeared. His late wife, Sara, had never used the stuff, nor did Jane or his friend Gladys Wyatt and he approved.

Arlie realized this was not Lara's usual sleekly groomed, polished exterior. "Had a hard night, did we?" Arlie muttered to himself and not without humour.

Then he shook his head, none of his business. Lately, he had been making an effort to keep his nose out of other people's petty affairs, especially now he had a bigger goal in mind. Change was possible, wasn't it, even when a man was sixty-eight?

Arlie took his familiar position behind the counter and waited.

From his angle he could see Mayor Ann Westcott exit her vehicle and come striding around the corner of the van. Her scowl was directed toward the window and Arlie felt it was aimed at him. She obviously didn't see Lara, and ran right into her, knocking the older woman back a couple of steps.

The impact made Ann drop the wad of paper she was carrying and also knocked the angry look off her face. "I'm sorry," Ann sputtered.

Arlie could hear the muffled apology, but it didn't look like it did any good.

"Jane, your sister's here," Arlie called back to his boss. Things were about to get interesting.

"Okay, thanks." Jane's words drifted in from the kitchen, but Arlie's attention was back on the exchange outside. He leaned forward, hand resting on the spotless counter to hear their words better. He wasn't snooping, just interested. The parking lot was public access, wasn't it?

"You stupid, git," Lara said sharply. She employed her elbows and round bulk to push past Ann. "Just get out of my way." She beat the younger woman to the door, leaving Ann to pick up her stream of paper. The banner was now on the ground, with one corner wet from a two-foot mud puddle by her rear right tire and turning brown.

"Uh oh," Arlie muttered, he was sure he recognized the stream of paper.

He refocused as Lara pulled the coffee shop door open. The bell over the door gave a flat clank, not its usual musical tinkle.

She briskly stalked up to the counter. "I want a large drip coffee, strong."

Arlie blinked at the abrupt woman's manner. "Sure. That'll be two-fifty, please," he said. "Coffee, cups, and lids are behind you along the north wall, under the windows along with the cream and sugar." His tone was clipped but not unfriendly.

Lara Finkle was a customer he reminded himself again, so he gave her a small, pleasant smile. He would be civil, even if she wasn't. Her involvement in an illicit affair with Musgrave Landing's former embezzling mayor, Tim Stanhope's, ended with Tim's murder. That was over two years ago.

Arlie knew it would be best if he could forget those events and set them aside. The murderer had been caught, and the whole episode resolved. Well, mostly.

He could hear Lara grind her teeth as she dug a hand into the bottom of her purse. Her reaction made his smile evolve into a grin. His good humour appeared to annoy her. She pulled out some change and threw the coins on the counter. Then, without any further words, she turned her back on him and made for the coffee station.

Quietly he gathered up the money. Sure, he could set his opinion of the woman aside. He counted the money. Like any small town, Lara's connection with Stanhope was certainly not going to be forgotten. He just shouldn't allow any of it to spill out

The change was sorted and dropped it into the cash register by the time Ann flung the red French door open in her usual way. The bell over the door tinkled as the restraining hinge did its job, stopping the door from being slammed against the wall. Arlie merely sighed at the determined expression on the slender, forty-something woman's face.

Lara, who now clutched a to-go cup of hot coffee, grabbed Ann by the arm as she entered the café. The older woman yanked the mayor to a halt. "Have you been talking to the police?"

"What?" Ann was totally nonplused by Lara grabbing her arm. She twisted her wrist and pulled free to remove the contact.

Lara dropped her hand, but moved forward to stand in front of Ann, blocking her path to the counter.

While Ann was younger and taller, Lara was much more aggressive. "Has there been any progress on finding the thief who's terrorizing the village? I was robbed last night." Anger and impatience salted her tone.

"No. Not that I know of, but the RCMP don't report to me." Ann took a step sideways from the belligerent other woman. She composed herself and put on her politician face. "I'm sorry to hear you've been robbed. When did this happen? What was taken?"

Lara snorted like she didn't believe Ann was sorry at all. "Either last night or early this morning. They got my–" she broke off as she clamped her mouth shut.

Arlie lifted his bushy salt and pepper eyebrows as he unabashedly listened in. Lara stopped mid-sentence either from emotion, or because she didn't want to share what had been stolen from her. Interesting.

Lara waved away her previous words and leaned in to scowl at Ann. "Never mind what they took. I want those criminals locked up, and I demand you do something to make it happen."

"I'm sorry, but you aren't the only person in the village who's had their property stolen. Maybe call the RCMP Detachment for an update or check their media profile." Ann suggested in a polished professional tone.

Lara pointed a scarlet-painted talon at the mayor. "Look, this situation has gone way beyond porch pirates. You should demand the cops report their progress to you. It's what they get paid for." She looked Ann up and down with a disgusted look on her face. "You could do your job better, you know. The village is being plagued by a gang of thieves. You need to demand the cops do more to catch them." Hot coffee slopped over the rim of her cup with her agitated movements, but Lara didn't seem to notice.

Arlie widened his eyes at Lara's words. Was Ann going to let that pass without comment? Well, he couldn't.

Arms folded across his chest he rocked back on his heels. "Because it's just that easy," he said, keeping the tone of his commentary even.

Lara cut her eyes to him but ignored his words.

Ann's glance darted over to him as well. She narrowed her eyes compressed her lips, and her fingers curled into the crumpled paper she held in her right hand. He could see her temper rising again from her flushed complexion. Arlie couldn't blame the mayor. At least not for the current crime wave anyway.

It appeared Lara wasn't done. "You are accountable, or should be, for this mess. We didn't have thieves running around the village when Tim was mayor."

"That's because, at that time, Tim Stanhope was the village's biggest thief," Ann said crisply.

Arlie laughed; he couldn't help himself. "Ha! She got you there."

The Lara turned her glare back on him, lifting her upper lip off her front teeth to snarl at him.

He kept going. "Everyone knows about the embezzlement and the fraud he committed against the provincial and municipal government. He stole money that belonged to the village. Tim ripped off us taxpayers so don't act so indignant."

"Exactly," Ann gave Arlie a nod before she continued. "Now, everyone needs to keep a close watch on their properties. I suggest you do the same. Someone will see something soon, they'll report it, and the police will catch the people responsible for the thefts." Ann made to go around Lara. "Have you reported your theft to the RCMP, Lara?"

"You are completely useless; you do know that?" Lara said into the younger woman's face and then brushed by Ann. She swung the door open and stalked out of the cafe. In the parking lot, Lara gunned her engine did a 180 degree turn to put her car in the queue for the ferry.

Ann threw an irritated glance in Lara's direction as she turned away. She expelled a frustrated breath and then Ann turned to lock her hard gaze on Arlie.

Oh, not good.

Chapter Two

Jane's sister narrowed her eyes at Arlie. Jaw thrust out, she marched up to the counter. Her pixie-cut brown hair stood out from her head like a bristling cat's fur as her glare pinned Arlie in place.

"What do you know about this 'Coming Soon, Chalet Coffee' sign?" She flung the crumpled paper at him. The torn paper bounced off the bib of his black apron and landed on the clean counter dusting it with sand.

Arlie wrinkled his nose in distaste.

"This banner was hanging above the door on the new pump house building." Menace permeated each one of Ann's words. "I know it was you!" She stabbed her index finger at him.

Arlie shifted his feet but managed to keep his expression natural. He ignored the signage and picked up the spare forty cents Lara had left behind. Playing for time, he dumped the coins into the Ethel Crawly Beautification Project jar.

Slowly, he turned back to Ann. "There's a new coffee shop coming to the village? Jane won't be happy about that," he said innocently and picked up a new white cleaning cloth from the stack under the counter and edged back along its length to

15

make his way over to the espresso machine. The half wall was between them now and offered the old man the illusion of safety.

"Don't be obtuse," Ann said through clenched teeth as she followed him and stood opposite. She had to rise upon tip-toe to glare at the older man. "I know you're behind this misinformation campaign." She stabbed her index finger at him again. "I know it's you. You put these signs up on the new facility." She accused. "You're behind the attack on my record as mayor, aren't you?"

Arlie ignored her last question as he polished residue from the machine's chrome. While it was true Ann had used her authority as mayor to support her pet cause, the ECBP. She hadn't actually used her position for her own gain. Not like Tim Stanhope had. All the funds raised for Ann's deceased aunt's charity were accounted for. The members of the charity board published a financial statement in the local paper once a year. The board followed the example of the village council regarding the budget– transparency and accountability. Ann, as mayor, was completely honest, and there was no disputing that fact.

So too, the mayor and village council ensured full reporting to the residences of Musgrave Landing. Statements were issued annually pertaining to any moneys the village collected or spent including grants and taxes collected. But still, there needed to be some discretion and limits put in place on where the collected money was spent. It was that type of wasteful spending that spawned the banner to appear on the brand-new pump house. As well as the logical assumption that increased taxes would follow.

Finally, Arlie shifted his eyes to look at her. "I've heard the council thinks they can add the expense of those old growth cedar beams, flashy black granite facade, and paved parking lot for the new pump house to our property taxes. The result being everyone's rates will go through the roof." He folded his arms across his chest, but kept the rest of his expression neutral, waiting for her response. From the widening of her eyes, he gauged he'd hit the mark.

"The municipality chose those building materials to ensure the building is in keeping with its surroundings. Musgrave Landing village council had little control over how the auxiliary pump house was constructed or how it was finished. That said, I like how the facility turned out and so do many other people."

"Right," Arlie said with heavy distain. "Wait until they get their tax bills." He moved on to wiping down the countertops. "Still has to be paid for and most who like it, haven't considered that the Muni doesn't pay for anything. All funds spent are taxpayer supplied. Even grant money."

Ann waved Arlie's words away. "Of course, we have to pay our share, but the village needed the auxiliary pumping station. We had enough problems last year when the water had to be shut off to fix the access from the river. We need a secondary drinking water source."

Jane entered from the kitchen. She stepped around Arlie and slid a rack of chocolate chip cookies into the display case. The sisters shared the same dark-brown hair, but Jane's was long and braided, in contrast to Ann's. She had green eyes to her elder sister's dark brown ones and Jane was also shorter and curvier. But, in Arlie's opinion, who would trust a skinny baker? She was also married to his son Jack, and he couldn't be happier in Jack's choice of bride. Jane was fairly close to perfect in Arlie's mind.

"Yes, the new facility is a good thing," Jane said entering into the conversation. "You were elected on the promise of spending accountability, among others. If property taxes go up for residents, taxes will go up for businesses too." She closed the sliding door on the display case and walked up to the counter. "That said, what happened to all the money Tim Stanhope embezzled? I thought the RCMP got the funds back." She picked up the soiled paper from the counter, opened it to read the banner, and then tossed the lot into the garbage by the sink.

Arlie wiped up the sand from the counter and dropped the soiled cloth in the laundry basket inside the kitchen door.

"Not, all of it," Ann said. She heaved a sigh and tugged down the jacket of her powder-blue suit. "Some grant funds are still not accounted for."

Jane shook her head as she washed her hands.

Arlie grunted at this too. At least Jane's presence appeared to take some of the wind out of her sister's sails.

Ann ran an agitated hand through her short-cropped hair. "The bulk of the money they returned to us has been spent to fix infrastructure and the roads, just as I promised. But, yes, the village will have to contribute a big chunk of money for the cost of the new pump house. And once we know the total cost, taxes may have to be raised." She gave a one shoulder shrug.

"An extravagant amount I'm betting." Arlie piped up.

Ann merely compressed her lips, not looking at him or answering him.

Like every politician ever elected. With a dismissive sniff, Arlie began the process for creating a caramel-vanilla latte.

Jane leaned a hip against the counter in her usual spot and folded her arms. "How much is still missing?" the café owner asked, tipping her head in inquiry.

"I don't actually know, not exactly." Her sister said over the hiss and spit of the coffee machine. "Possibly half a million dollars, maybe more, Celina would know." Celina Nickels, a professional accountant, was re-elected councillor at the same time Ann was chosen as mayor. Celina held the position of treasurer for the village.

Jane locked eyes with her sister. "Is yelling at my father-in-law about some silly sign a symptom of your frustration with the village finances?"

Arlie blinked at how Jane stressed her relationship with him, and he felt a spark of warmth which triggered a small smile. He shifted his eyes between the sisters as his machine worked. With her calm and reasonable tone, one would think Jane was the elder, certainly wiser of the two.

Ann looked over at Arlie and met his gaze. "Yes, I guess so." She released another sigh as her eyes skittered away.

Arlie chanced a glance at Jane, no reaction.

"I think that sign was a harmless prank," Jane said while she gave her sister a steady look. "It appears to me to be a protest by some villagers against the project's management and procurement decisions, not as a slight against you. Besides, why would Arlie do such a thing? And when would he have the time, he's much too busy working here and lately, helping Gladys move into her new condo."

"You think so?" Ann gave Arlie a hard look, like she didn't quite believe it.

Arlie had the feeling she wasn't buying it, so he tried to look as innocent as possible, adding a gentle smile for the mayor.

"Yes," Jane said firmly, but there was a warning in the simple word. He was touched again by Jane's defense. He also experienced a small flash of guilt but got over it quickly.

Ann breathed in through her nose and turned to look at the older man again. "I'm sorry, Arlie."

He lifted one shoulder in response as he poured flavoured steamed milk and strong coffee into a cardboard to-go cup. He was glad Jane knew how to handle her sister's volatile moods. Artists, who could figure them out?

Arlie finished the drink off with a stylized heart in milk foam. "No hard feelings," he said and moved to place the hot beverage on the counter in front of his daughter-in-law's sister.

Ann lifted her sculpted eyebrows at the coffee.

"On the house," Jane said and placed a lid on top before she slid the cardboard cup across to her sibling.

"Thanks." Ann wrapped long fingers around the latte and gave him and her sister a nod.

"No problem." Arlie said as Ann made her way out of the café and back to her vehicle.

The two watched Jane's sister get into her minivan. She started the old vehicle, backed out of the lot, turned, and drove up High Street toward the village office.

"You have to stop." Jane flattened her lips as she shifted her gaze to look at him.

Arlie kept his eyes on the van's taillights disappear. "I only held the ladder."

Chapter Three

There was a knock on the kitchen door behind Jane and Arlie. They both turned as the delivery entrance door opened.

"Hello. Hello!" Gladys Wyatt called out to them.

"Hey there, Gladys." Arlie greeted her; his mood immediately lifted.

"I've got your bread order, Jane." The stocky older woman carried in a bright blue bread rack containing a dozen unsliced loaves. Her small, compact body carried some muscle even for a senior citizen. The muscle was no doubt from lugging around the industrial bread racks for the past decade.

"Thanks so much, Gladys," Jane said and moved forward.

Arlie briskly strode pasted his daughter-in-law and into the kitchen to relieve his friend of her burdens. "I'll give you a hand," he said to Gladys.

She bestowed a sunny smile on him.

He felt his ears redden from the attention but ignored the reaction. He wasn't ready to tell Gladys the sparkle in her blue eyes made his day.

"I've got this, Jane." Arlie took the rack from Gladys.

The bell over the café door tinkled as three people entered the coffee shop. A man, a woman, and a boy around twelve. The boy made a beeline for the treats display case.

"Thanks, Arlie. Gladys' envelope is in the slot." Jane turned away to serve the new customers.

"Thanks, I could use the help." Grey-shot light-brown curls bounced as she moved.

"Humph," Arlie grunted and tried to blank his expression. Although he couldn't suppress the spring in his step as he followed her out through the adjacent door where the vertical freezer was housed. The two worked companionably together to load this first batch of bread onto the shelves of the unit.

"Did you want to leave any out?" Gladys held up the last two loafs of multigrain.

"Yeah, good call. We'll leave those on the counter for the lunch rush."

Gladys lined up the fresh loaves neatly on the counter and Arlie followed. He carried the now empty rack as Gladys opened the kitchen door to get the next load.

Arlie paused to extract Gladys' envelop from the vintage 1950's wall-hung letter holder and tucked it into the top pocket of his apron.

He caught up with her in the delivery parking spot at the rear of the cafe. They walked around the back of Gladys' forest-green, faux-wood panelled station wagon. The rear gate was open.

The car was parked in the new unloading zone Arlie had designed, and with the help of his son Jack, had made happen. New asphalt paving kept the mud out of the kitchen and the three parking slots allow room for the delivery catering van Jane had purchased as well as a temporary space for deliveries.

Since the back lot had been created, the tiny front parking lot was always accessible for customers. Sometime this fall, they had plans to have the front parking lot paved as well and that would be the end of his battle with mud when it rained. This being the Pacific Northwest, it rained a lot.

"ARE YOU ALL SETTLED into your new place yet?"

Gladys had backed into the space and unloading was simple. Heavy duty racks of whole wheat and rye bread were waiting along with bags of fresh crusty rolls. The car's interior smelled like a bakery, much better than any commercial air fresher in her opinion. Her small business kept her occupied and kept the citizens of Musgrave Landing well stocked with delicious homemade breads and buns.

Arlie stacked the racks, one on top of the other, and slid them across the open tailgate.

"I'm getting there, it's a work in progress. Thanks again for your help moving me. Thank Jack again for me too. I want to have all of you over for dinner, soon," she said happily. "How is Saturday for you all?"

"I like the sound of that. I'll check with Jane, but I'm betting she and Jack are free."

"Good, I thought we could make a real dinner party out of it, like a housewarming." She glanced up at him with an excited smile. "My granddaughter will be joining us too."

"Right, you had her with you on Friday for lunch." Arlie said as they moved back toward the open door.

"Yes, she's staying with me, or was, while she gets her feet back under her."

"Was?"

"Maisy's dog sitting and minding the condo for my neighbour across the hall, Mathew Wilkes, at the moment."

Arlie nodded. "Ah, I see."

"Let me know if you hear of any jobs that come open. She's looking for work."

"What kind of work?"

"Anything, really, she needs to start making money."

"You have enough room for all of us in your new apartment?"

"Oh yes, it's true the condo is a smaller space overall compared to my old house, but the kitchen is much bigger and better laid out for cooking and entertaining. I think it's the open landscape design that allows for it."

"I'm glad your move has worked out so well." He shifted the bread trays to get a better grip.

"I like the apartment." Her smile faded a bit. "Although the condo board is something else, so many rules, but I'm getting used to it."

Arlie nodded as they reached the back kitchen door, and she held it open. "Give me a couple of seconds to unload these."

"I'll help you." She joined him in the kitchen. The fragrance of fresh baking complemented the aroma of fresh coffee. Gladys breathed it in. She'd always like the café back when Ethel Crawley had run it, but now Jane had taken the business to a new level. A lucky turn of events for Gladys and her bakery business, the day Jane asked her to start supplying bread products.

The pair exchanged shy smiles as they worked. Gladys couldn't think of any new topics to keep the conversations going. It was an odd feeling, being tongue-tied.

Once outside again, Arlie slid all three racks into the back of the station wagon and closed the rear gate for her.

"Thanks, Arlie. Well, I still have cinnamon buns to bake. The dough will be raised by the time I get back home. I should get going."

"Oh? Who are those for?" he asked carefully. "Are you adding to your product line?"

"No, I promised Maisy. They're her favourite."

"Ah." Arlie brightened. "You said your granddaughter was dog-sitting for Matthew Wilkes? How is Albert?"

Gladys gave Arlie a small smile. He put up a gruff front, but she knew her friend didn't mind admitting to having a soft spot for canines, most specifically his son's German shepherd, Vimy.

"Mending, poor pup. We can't figure out how he could have worked his way under the glass barrier to fall from the balcony. He's too chunky." Gladys sighed in empathy.

"He's an old dog too. It's surprising he survived at all."

"I know. Matthew was going to cancel his contract to stay home, but I volunteered Maisy to look after Albert this week. She was happy to help."

"Still, strange to think that after five months of living in the unit the dog only now figured out how to get over or around the balcony railing. What's Matthew going to do about that? He's on the ravine side of the building."

Gladys nodded. "He's had to Gerry-rigged a barricade out of wood to block the lower part. Not that Albert looks the least bit interested in going out on the balcony anymore. He stands in the living room to bark at the birds."

"I imagine not."

"He spends most of his day at my place. Maisy has a basket there for him."

"Heh," Arlie snorted. "How's the dog getting along with your cat?"

"There is an uncertain peace between Albert and Blofeld. So far, only glares and a tiny bit of growling exchanged between the two of them."

Something in Gladys' voice made Arlie frown. "What aren't you saying?"

Gladys glanced away to stare at her feet for a moment, and then finally looked up at him. Whatever she was about to say disturbed her. He waited and hoped she would confide in him. Gladys was his friend and he sensed something was troubling her.

"I live right across the hall from Matthew. I should have heard the poor thing."

"Only if you were at home. Who found Albert in the ravine?"

"Matthew did, after he got home from work and found the wee dog missing." She couldn't help the tears that pooled in her eyes. "I should have heard something. I feel so bad thinking about the poor dog was lying out there."

Arlie put an arm around her shoulders and gave her a quick hug. "It's okay, Glad," he said, his pet name for her. "Albert is fine now."

"I know." She dashed the tears away and took a breath.

"Have you heard about the thefts around the village?" Arlie asked, to change the subject. "You've still got all your patio furniture, don't you?" His question was gentle as he released her.

"Yes, I do. I keep my patio doors locked, too when I'm not in the condo. And the hallway door as well. I'm on the ground floor. I hope these feckless people are caught soon so we can go back to normal. Back to feeling safe in our community."

"Lara Finkle was in the café before you arrived. She said she'd been robbed. Did you hear about that?"

"No. When was this?" Gladys shook her head. "Did she say what was stolen?"

Arlie frowned. "No details, but I guess it happened last night or this morning, early. The thieves might have gotten wind of her involvement with Tim Stanhope. Probably figured she still had some of the stolen money lying around. It serves her right. She had to be involved with the crap Tim pulled. She had to be on the receiving end of some of the money. That's probably how she could afford to buy her condo, I bet."

"Now Arlie," Gladys said, placing a restraining hand on his arm. "I'm not Lara's friend either, but you have no proof she received any of the stolen funds. It was two years ago, for heaven's sake. You can't go around accusing people."

"I'm not, but I'm just saying what everyone else is thinking. What can she do, take away my birthday?" he snorted. "How did she buy that condo unit then?"

"She sold her house, like I did." Gladys raised her eyebrows reproachfully at him. "Who knows what she got for her property. Maybe she did very well and decided to downsize, again, like I did."

Arlie growled under his breath. Then he sighed. "Let's change the subject."

"Good idea."

"About Maisy, would she be interested working in the café? It would only be a few hours a day, during the noon rush, and only for the summer."

"I don't see why not. The café is a lovely place to work, that's for sure. I'll tell her to come by and see Jane." Gladys shone her smile on him.

"Good, I'll let Jane know Maisy might be interested. Tell her to come to the cafe as soon as she can. Jane plans to put an ad in the Village Voice for more help tomorrow. If she likes Maisy, and hires her, we won't have to do that."

"Will do."

"One last thing," Arlie said as she slid the envelope out of his top pocket and offered it to her. "Here's your payment for last week's deliveries." He handed her the missive and Gladys rewarded him with another smile.

"Thanks." She gestured with the envelope, and then tucked it carefully into the pocket of her red crocheted vest.

Arlie looked dramatically left, then right. "So, are you free for this evening?"

"What do you have in mind?" She coyly raised one eyebrow.

"Maybe a bit of ladder work."

"Really?" Gladys frowned "Already? We just put the last one up."

Arlie grimaced. "Ann had the banner torn down. She was here this morning, shaking her tiny fists at me."

"Can she prove you were involved?"

He snorted. "No, of course not." Then he grinned, looking pleased with himself. "I think my reputation has preceded me."

"No doubt." Gladys' tone was dry.

His eyes sparkled with mischief. "Want to help me put up another one?"

Gladys wrinkled her nose and grinned back at him. "Of course, I do."

Chapter Four

Gladys mentally reviewed her task list for the rest of the day as she drove the second-hand station wagon along the Coast Road. The oversized vehicle was a recent purchase. As her bakery business had picked up, it rapidly became apparent she needed more room to haul around the product for deliveries and her old sedan just didn't cut it anymore.

Fortunately for Gladys, Father Edward, a regular recipient of her Alpine loaves, heard about her need. On Coffee Sunday, two weeks ago he'd button-holed her.

"Gladys, I have a tip for you." The seventy-something priest popped up at her workstation in the parish kitchen. She was busy cutting up a raspberry-rhubarb crumble into serving sizes.

"Ah, in regard to what, Father?" She slipped a slice of the desert onto a plate for him and slid it across the counter.

"I heard you were looking for a vehicle for bakery deliveries." The white-haired man in his black suit picked up the desert and selected a fork from the stack. "Oh, this looks good. Is it yours?"

"No, Helen Eberly made this crumble. It's quite lovely." She raised an eyebrow at him in enquiry. She had to move this along. Helen's desert was very popular, and the line was growing longer by the minute.

"Yes, yes. Anyway, I heard Moffatt Funeral Services were looking to sell off a late model Forester station wagon. Kevin has cleared out the garage and wants the old vehicle gone before he takes delivery of the new hearse."

Gladys gave the priest a doubtful look. She was sure she knew where he was going with this. The station wagon had been the old hearse and she wasn't sure she wanted any part of it.

As if guessing her thoughts, Father Edward smiled. "It's merely a car, Gladys."

She cut another slice and handed it off to Debbie Milley, standing behind the priest, next in line. "Don't forget this." Gladys moved the bowl of whipped cream forward.

"Oh, thanks." Debbie helped herself.

The priest added cream to his after Debbie moved away. "The funeral director said the car's never been driven over fifty kilometres an hour, and I can believe it."

"Me too, it was the hearse." Gladys served the next slice to Monica Troendle. "Thanks for the information."

He gestured to her with his fork. "It's certainly worth a look."

"Yes, you're probably right," Gladys allowed.

Father Edward nodded and darted off in the direction Gail James, the CWL president.

The priest had been right. The Forrester was in excellent condition. The car's low mileage had caught Gladys' interest too, at under fifty thousand kilometers. However, what sold her on the car were the rollers installed in the back where the rear seats would have been. Plus, the way the back gate opened completely flat for easy loading and unloading.

Micky, Gladys' late husband, would have been proud of the deal she'd wrung out of Kevin Moffatt for the station wagon. Her husband had taught her well

"You drive a hard bargain, Gladys. You're also the only person to actually come over and see it." Kevin admitted as they shook hands. "People can be so superstitious."

Gladys certainly was not. She didn't fear the dead either.

That deal, along with the money she'd gotten for the sale of her old sedan, had been satisfactory in Gladys' mind.

A quick glance at the analog dashboard clock told her it was nearing eight o'clock. As soon as Maisy dropped over for breakfast, Gladys would tell her about the opportunity to work at Jane's café. She wished she could help Maisy as easily as she'd fixed her own transportation problem.

If she got the part-time café job, Maisy would be earning for her future. The sooner her granddaughter got some money put by, the closer the girl would be to getting herself sorted out. Maybe then Maisy could figure out a career path.

The initial plan had been for Maisy to sell her grandmother's baking at the farmers' markets. Helping her granddaughter out was worth splitting her profits for a month or two. They'd figure something out with the markets and the café job later.

The morning sun was already gaining strength and warmed the interior of the vehicle. The heat felt good on her skin, but rapidly became too hot. Gladys lowered her window to allow some of the cooler salty air into the car.

Driving the old wagon wasn't a chore, she enjoyed the trips. Most of her deliveries were a short distance from her condo building on the shore of the Samsum Narrows anyway, so she wasn't required to travel very far.

Still, days like today were the best, pay day. Her left hand absently drifted to the envelope in her vest pocket. The paper crinkled faintly, and Gladys smiled with satisfaction.

Thinking about the cheque she carried, she'd have to adjust her schedule again. A trip to the bank needed to be inserted into today's timetable somewhere. Maybe now she'd start getting ahead of her expenses. The common element fees attached to owning a new unit and the last special assessment were her main worries. She hoped the building's initial construction problems were behind them.

Gladys very much liked her spacious apartment. The huge kitchen had sold it for her, along with the option to have dual ovens. A must for her cottage bakery business. The place was also comfortable, and she welcomed not having a yard to maintain. Gardening hadn't ever been her thing. Micky was the gardener and the entire yard of their former home, front and back, showed it. Her husband had grown everything from robust fruit trees, a vegetable garden, to delicate orchids. She didn't miss the garden, but she did miss Micky.

She had known she'd never do justice to her late husband's work. Nor did she want to even try. It was better to sell her home to the young couple with one child already, and one on the way. The rambling old house needed a family. It was too large and quiet for one middle-aged widow watching a sprawling yard and garden slowly get out of hand.

So too, was trying to find someone to do repairs she couldn't handle, yet another thing Gladys didn't like to deal with. Handling trade people, or even the plumber to replace the water filtration system, had always been Micky's job.

While it was true, their son Malcolm could help, and he did when he visited, it was her responsibility. Malcolm had the skills taught to him by his father, but living in Victoria and working in Vancouver, meant he traveled a lot. Her son had his own home and challenges without worrying about his mother's domestic issues. No way did Gladys want to add to Malcolm and Sharon's load.

It wasn't difficult to see that a smaller home, with less maintenance was a good idea. After a year of living solo, she decided it was time to move on and time to try something new. The condo idea seemed like a good fit, at least at the time she'd bought into the building. Who could have planned for the events that would follow?

Gladys lifted her chin and took a deep breath. She'd call Malcolm on Sunday. Just to check in and speak to him about his daughter.

Getting a hold of her son was never easy. She knew Maisy texted her parents. But texting wasn't something Gladys preferred. She wanted to hear her son's voice. Usually, she left a message and followed up with an email. Eventually they would connect for a call. The process could sometimes take days.

For now, Gladys pushed these thoughts away, she had work to do. She still had one more order to fill today. This one was for the Smuggler's Inn, a bed and breakfast in Whisky Corner, some ten minutes from the village. If she timed it right, she could make the quick trip to the neighbouring hamlet while her next set of loaves were rising.

"Count your blessings, old girl. Things are getting better." She murmured to herself, slowing the car to avoid a squirrel running across the road.

Her granddaughter lived close by now, practically living with her, and something to be thankful for.

The black furry creature scampered up the closest Sitka spruce tree and disappeared. Gladys allowed the car to speed up again.

Thoughts of Maisy made Gladys smile. The girl was like a burst of sunshine on a cloudy day. Although she needed to figure out what she wanted to do with her life, but at nineteen there was still lots of time.

Not half a block away from her home, Gladys passed a dark navy panelled van parked across the road from her building. Heath's Plumbing was stencilled on the side.

It was parked next to the entrance to the marina her building overlooked. "Odd place to park," she muttered to herself, and then slowed the station wagon. There was a lag in the steering, and she had to plan ahead to turn the big car.

Gladys frowned as the condo building came into view. A rusted brown, late model Plymouth currently blocked the approach to the driveway. She was forced to come to a stop at the rear of the vehicle. The driver didn't take any notice of her car directly behind him. He merely continued to sit where he was. His head was turned, and he appeared to be intent on the building.

To her right, the new condo complex rested on the side of the mountain, surrounded by terraced gardens. Gladys' apartment was on the east side, 102, facing the water and mountains. Her patio overlooked the marina, with a spectacular view of the bay.

Curiously, the car in front of Gladys was running. Maybe he was looking for someone who lived in her building. Could it be the driver was confused because there was no address posted? Nor was there a street sign as yet, although her deed did say the address was 636 Coast Road.

She knew the address did not show up on any map app either, but then the location was not yet a year old. It took time for technology to catch up. She doubted any big tech companies would drive the village streets to update their maps any time soon.

People had just begun moving into the units five months ago. Only one apartment on the second floor remained empty.

Gladys had spoken to Ann Westcott about a street sign and written a formal request to the council. No signage meant getting deliveries was terribly difficult. Until there was, she would have to continue to pick up her own baking supplies from Vancouver Island.

Patiently, she waited for the man to make up his mind. Was he pulling in or moving on? To prod him, she flipped on her signal light to show she wanted to turn. He still didn't move his car or even glance in the rear-view mirror.

Gladys sighed at the delay and drummed her fingers on the steering wheel. "This is getting ridiculous." She could see the back of the driver's bald head. He was wearing a dark brown windbreaker and sat hunched over the wheel as he looked through the windshield at the property. She didn't recognize the car and glanced at his licence plate, British Columbia. So, maybe not a tourist, but definitely not a local resident either.

After waiting one more full minute, Gladys tapped her horn. Now he turned his head and looked back at her through the rear window.

She couldn't read his reaction from this distance, but he gunned the engine loudly and the decrepit vehicle sped noisily away. She watched the car turn sharply at the corner. He was headed away from the village.

Gladys gave a one shoulder shrug and took her foot off the brake, turned the wheel, and rolled down the drive to her parking spot by the back door.

It saved her a few dollars by not taking a slot under the building. Still, when the rains came in the fall she might regret it, though every dime saved meant she could afford to keep the condo. Besides, the old station wagon was tough enough to stay out in the elements.

Micky never parked their car inside either. "Garages are made for working on cars, not for storing them," he'd tell her gruffly. As an automobile mechanic, Micky would know.

Her lips formed a wry smile, thinking about her late husband. He'd have hated the condo. Gladys put the car into park and shut off the engine. She got out of the car to look up at the two-story exterior. Some days, she could agree with him, but not today.

Chapter Five

Large, lead-lined cathedral windows sparkled in the sunshine. Their sheer size allowed an abundance of sunlight to penetrate each of the eight apartments. The white clapboard exterior and arched windows made the multi-unit building look very upscale. Its appearance was helped by the flowerbeds out front and here in the back. The terraced levels overflowed with red, white, and pink roses. Their buds released a delicate fragrance.

Norm Gorlitz was in charge of the grounds. He and his late wife, Carol, had been part of her and Micky's circle of friends back in the day. Same as Arlie and his wife, Sara, had been. The men would discuss all aspects of growing roses, lilies, and orchids for hours while the group of them played cards. She missed Carol's dry sense of humour, and Sara's ability to see the bright side of every situation too. So many people she'd know were gone. The thought made her throat tighten.

Ah, well. She cleared her throat and looked around but didn't see Norm. He was employed to maintain the gardens, cut the grass, and oversee outside repairs. One of the battles she'd won against Enid Lindquist and Dwayne Davis. As part of the condo board, they wanted to hire a service, not someone local to manage the outside areas. Dwayne tried to bully her and Matthew into doing things his way.

Matthew was not intimidated by anything. "Big companies don't care a twiddle for small customers like us. If there's a big snowfall in winter, we will have to wait ages for someone to come and clear our road access. Norm Gorlitz is a local guy. He'd know who to call right away in that situation." Matthew had stood up to Dwayne. Her younger neighbour was a great ally.

"We'll put it to a vote." Enid thought she had them, but in the end, Linda Leechie and Freddie Freeman sided with hiring Norm, four to three. Lara never attended meetings. The third vote belonged to the company who still held the unsold condo. Enid had their proxy.

At least Gladys and Matthew had won that battle. She knew as a retired veteran, Matthew was still bitter over losing the vote to fly the Canadian flag from his balcony. They'd have to bring the issue up again before Canada Day. Maybe she could make Freddie and Linda see sense and vote along with her and Matthew. And if it came to it, Gladys planned to approach Lara Finkle. If she would not vote with allowing the patriotic symbol, then at least abstain and not allow Enid to use Lara's proxy. Something Enid pursued after losing the groundskeeper vote.

All in all, Gladys liked her new home. The extra work and the politics were worth it to live here.

As she walked around the car to the rear, she noted the globe cedar shrubs Norm had begun to plant this week. Only two were left in their netting next to a pair of holes already dug.

He'd made good progress. The shrubs partially hid the walkway lighting fixtures and made a nice backdrop for the flowers.

Usually, Gladys could make out Norm puttering around somewhere. He was easy to spot because of the red, blue, and white slouch hat his daughter had given him for his sixty-sixth birthday last year. If Norm was outside, the hat was perched on his head and served as a beacon. He wasn't about at the moment.

The interior of 636 Coast Road was Enid Lindquist's responsibility. She managed the building and organized contractors, similar to Norm for the outside. On a new structure such as this, there shouldn't be many problems, or at least one would think so. Unfortunately, there seemed to be an endless list of things not covered under the building's warranty. Enid, a retired high school principal, acted like she answered only to the building owner. Some faceless corporation named Pink Brick. As far as Gladys knew, no one had ever met anyone from Pink Brick, with the possible exception of Enid and Leslie Whipple, Musgrave Landing's only real estate agent.

In reality, the condo board was supposed to be in charge. However, Enid held the two extra votes, as well as her own and welded her power like a club. She and Dwayne colluded on every issue.

As soon as the last unit was sold the corporation responsible for commissioning the build would no longer be in the picture. Maybe then getting things done with the condo board would be much smoother.

Until then, Enid was cock of the walk. Or was that the hen of the walk?

She opened the rear gate and hefted the bread racks out of the station wagon. A mortgage at her age, what had she been thinking? If it were only the bank payments, she'd have been fine. Unfortunately, there were also common element fees. Charges levied on each unit owner which applied to upkeep for the whole property. These she had not factored in when she had purchased the apartment. Then there were the extra expenses due to special assessments for repairs to the building too, the costs killed her nest egg.

The unit owners should sue the builder, but Pink Brick wouldn't allow it. Enid reported to them at the last meeting. Well, Gladys had plans to change their minds on that score but hadn't worked out a plan as of yet. Fingers crossed there would be no more plumbing issues with the second floor in the meantime.

She locked the vehicle. You couldn't be too careful, what with the thieves running around. Who knew what they'd steal next? She took the paved walkway to the back door, carrying the empty racks.

The glass and metal portal swung open as she approached. Two young men stepped out. Both appeared to be in their mid-twenties. They were dressed in jean shorts and loose-fitting T-shirts. The pair blinked at her for a second, looking mildly dazed.

"Let me get the door for you." The sandy-haired one on the left said, like he'd just woken up. Maybe it was the bedhead and that made her think that. He held the door wide for her all the same.

Gladys gifted him with a smile. "Thank you." It was nice the boys were polite. As she passed the pair, she couldn't help but notice the pungent aroma coming off both of them. Ah well, marijuana was legal and who was she to judge, but glad they weren't smoking it in the foyer.

"No problem." The young fellow released the door, so it slowly closed, and they wandered down the driveway toward the main road.

There was a man in his middle fifties standing at the elevator.

"Hi, Freddie." Gladys strolled past the second-floor resident who lived in unit 204. From a distance Freddie's wiry reddish-brown hair made him look younger than he was. A closer inspection showed his parted hair, a bit stringy, was doing a poor job of covering the bald patch on the back of his head. Freddie's face was etched with dozens of tiny laugh lines, but then he was a smoker, and that vice aged a person.

He turned and shifted heavy-lidded brown eyes to her. "Hey, Gladys. Do you need any help with those?" Freddie stepped closer and gestured to the bread racks. His jeans and rugby shirt hung loose on his lanky frame. One thing about her neighbours, most were friendly and helpful. Like a miniature community inside the village.

Gladys' nose twitched as she reached her door. Freddie too, had a pungent odor about him. Still, she smiled her thanks. "No thanks, I'm good." She set the load down by her door and dug for her keys.

The elevator pinged and the doors slid open. "See you later then." Freddie sauntered forward and disappeared inside. The doors slid closed.

Across the hallway, the apartment door of 104 opened and Maisy Wyatt stepped out. "Hey Grandma, I thought that was you." Albert, the Jack Russell terrier, squirted past Maisy's feet and danced forward. He still limped but the cast had come off yesterday and the brown and black dog seemed to be regaining his equilibrium.

Gladys smiled at her granddaughter. "Good morning, dear." She turned back to unlock her door. "Are you ready for breakfast?"

"I am."

"Yes, yes, hello, Albert." Gladys gave the enthusiastic little dog a quick pat, and then leaned down to pick up the racks.

"Hey, I've got those." Maisy took up the racks and waited for her grandmother to open the door.

"Thank you, my girl." Gladys quickly opened the door. "I have news for you too."

At almost twenty years old, Maisy Wyatt was tall, slender, and full of energy. The curly hair she got from her grandmother and father was naturally light blonde and gave her oval face a softer look. Her amber-coloured eyes displayed intelligence and interest. The golden skin tone, she got from her mother. The girl was a beauty, but not vain about it and that was a credit to her parents.

Maisy had done very well in high school, graduating with high honours, which was at odds with her current situation. She didn't think she was university material and had no idea what to do for a career. Maisy completed one semester of language arts at UBC in Vancouver and hated every moment of it. Malcolm and Shirley were not thrilled with this quitter attitude or the waste of the high tuition fees. However, not everyone got on well at university.

To relieve some of the family tension, Gladys had suggested Maisy come to her for the summer. Her intention was to help Maisy figure out her goals and make a plan.

Although university was not cheap, Gladys' son and daughter-in-law were working professionals and could pay the costs for their only child. Malcolm was a software engineer for a tech company, and Sharon worked in middle management for the BC government. Both made decent money. They could afford their daughter's education, but that wasn't the point. This was exactly what Malcolm had said in a phone call to his mother over a month ago when they'd made the arrangements.

"Maisy needs to focus on a skill or profession. Something so that when she's done, she can earn a living and be a contributing member of society. It's a parent's job to make their kids independent. Like you and Dad did for me."

"Yes, but something that will make her happy too." Gladys had countered.

"First a job, and then a career. She'll find happiness along the way, like I did." Gladys' son said firmly.

Her lips twitched at this memory. Maybe she and Micky had made Malcom too independent. Was that even possible? Still, it was best to separate the parents from their young adult for few weeks. Time away would help reduce the stress in their relationship and hopefully, allow Maisy time to figure out what to do.

In Gladys' mind, Maisy needed to work for a year to learn a few things. Just as well Gladys' neighbour, Matthew Wilkes, needed someone to look after his dog. This was Maisy's first employment, ever. The fact had taken Gladys by surprise when her granddaughter mentioned it. One didn't learn the value of a dollar and how to work overnight. Hopefully the café job might help in more ways than mere money.

Albert excitedly circled their feet as they entered Gladys' apartment. A quick look confirmed her white Persian was up on his cat tree in the back of the living room next to the patio doors. Blofeld watched Albert trot into the condo through green eyes narrowed to mere slits

"Something for you too, Albert, but you have to behave yourself." Gladys pointed an index finger warningly at the wee dog. Immediately Albert froze vibrating in place. No doubt thinking this was a game of some sort. "No growling at Blofeld."

The little dog gave one quick bark and darted to the right of the entranceway. He ran ahead straight to the cat's food dishes inside the utility room door.

"Sorry, he's already eaten." Maisy put down the racks and made to go after the dog.

Gladys waved away her concern. "He's fine. Let him have what's left in the bowl."

"I should bring his dishes with me in the morning." Maisy placed the bread racks in their place by the door. "It doesn't seem to matter he was already fed." She had her hands on her slim hips as she looked down at the animal. He looked innocently back up at her since he'd already inhaled the cat's dry food.

"He's a dog, it's what they do, no worries. Blofeld eats pretty early, so he's had his fill."

Without being asked, Maisy took a cleaning spray bottle out of the cupboard in the utility room and a clean cloth to wipe down the racks. This made them ready for the next delivery.

"Maisy, you are a treasure." Gladys put fresh water in a bowl and put it on the floor in the utility room for the dog. She then rescued the rest of her cat's food container from Albert's seeking nose. He gave her a sheepish look then noticed the water and dived in.

"It's the least I can do. I know there are cinnamon buns waiting for me here somewhere." She cleaned the bottom rack first.

"I'll just pre-heat the oven and we will have them with butter, fruit, and fresh coffee." She flicked on the coffee maker and went to the sink to wash her hands.

Maisy placed the clean racks side-by-side. "Awesome. You said something about news?"

"Oh, yes. You know the café by the ferry?" She grabbed a clean towel and dried her hands.

"Jane's Eats and Treats? Where we had lunch when I arrived?" Maisy moved on to the second rack.

"That's it. Would you be interested in working there part-time? Arlie Birch told me they're looking for help."

Maisy straightened and stared wide-eyed at her grandmother. "I...I, uh." Fear clouded her usually clear blue eyes.

"You can do it, my girl. Arlie and Jane are wonderful people and will train you on everything you need to know. It'll be just a few hours a day, and only for the summer, but at least it's a steady wage." Gladys glanced away for a moment and pushed some buttons on the lower built-in oven. She wanted to give Maisy a moment to think about the job offer. The digital display gave her a couple of beeps as she turned back to her granddaughter.

Gladys noticed Maisy had a tight grip on the cleaning cloth and twisted the cloth between her hands. "Tell me what you're thinking."

Maisy blinked at the moisture gathering in her eyes. "I'd have to wait on customers, strangers. What if I did something wrong?"

"You own up, apologize, and keep working." Gladys kept a steady gaze on the girl. "Maisy, people who don't make mistakes, don't do anything."

Maisy swallowed and compressed her lips into a straight line and gave her grandmother a tiny shake of her head. "I can't. I hardly know those people." The girl's confidence level was in need of a boost.

Gladys flattened her lips into a straight line. This was what came from not allowing teenagers to have after school jobs. Small jobs meant if you made mistakes, the missteps would be too small to matter in the long run. You could learn from those mistakes and be ready to take on bigger things when you became an adult.

Her daughter-in-law's word came back to Gladys. "I want Maisy to enjoy her summers. There's plenty of time to work when she's older." Sharon had meant well for Maisy, but now the girl's self-assurance was shaky when it came to new responsibilities. She was fearful of the unknown.

"Maisy, you are smart and a hard worker, you will do well. Also, Arlie asked me to ask you. He thought you'd be good at it, so you must have made a good impression." Okay, a white lie, but for the greater good.

The young girl blinked at her grandmother, surprised by these words. "Mr. Birch? Oh."

"Yes," Gladys picked up the cleaned dough hook from the draining rack and attached it to the mixer. She avoided Maisy's gaze. She fiddled with the machine settings in the brief silence. The girl was bright, helpful, and had a sunny nature, she'd do well working at the café.

"Okay, yeah."

Gladys looked back at her granddaughter with a pleased smile.

Maisy straightened her spine. "I'd be interested in the café job." An uncertain frown still clouded her expression. "What do I do now? How does the interview thing work?"

Relieved Maisy agreed to give the job a try, Gladys gave her granddaughter a wink. "It's all going to be very simple. After breakfast, change into walking shorts and a collared T-shirt. Then bike down to the café to talk to Jane Birch. She's expecting you."

"Okay." The girl nodded and took a calming breath. "This is my first job interview." Even thought she was still hesitant; Gladys gave Maisy points for moving forward anyway. "What do I say?"

"I'm sure Jane will do most of the talking, but ask her what she needs you to do. What the hours of work are, and how much training you can expect."

Maisy nodded again and put the cleaning cloth in the laundry hamper and spray solution bottle in its spot in the utility cupboard. "Do I ask how much she's going to pay me?" she asked when she re-emerged.

"Usually, they tell you that near the end of the conversation. But if she doesn't, yes, you can ask. Leave it till the end though."

"What about Albert?"

They both looked at the dog. He'd found a comfortable spot on the carpet in the sun and was stretched out on his belly. He lifted his head at the sound of his name.

"Leave him here with me. He'll be fine. If I go out, I'll put him in Matthew's apartment. I'm usually not gone longer than half an hour at most. It will be easy for me to adjust deliveries around your working hours."

"That's not really fair to you, Grandma. I agreed to watch him for Matthew." Maisy sounded doubtful.

"Albert is no trouble. I like his company. Besides, I'll get chores out of you in exchange."

Now Maisy grinned at her grandmother. "Deal."

Gladys nodded at her granddaughter, "Good." The oven beeped again, and she opened the door to slide the sheet of buns in.

Chapter Six

I t was almost noon when a low shout drew Gladys' attention from her phone call. A door slammed, followed by cursing. Angry voices emanated from the hallway.

Albert barked at the loud noises or possibly the emotion behind them. Gladys covered her end of the phone. "Hush, Albert." The small dog hadn't been the same since his accident, he was easily startled and not yet ready to deal with the unexpected. "Sorry, Casey what were you saying?"

Casey Pebbles was the owner of the Smuggler's Inn. He'd called to increase his bread order now that he was fully booked for the week. While the bookings might be part of the reason, Gladys wasn't fooled. Casey loved a good gossip and there had been no chance to visit earlier when she's dropped off his initial order. He'd been busy seeing to his new guests. Gladys figured out from Casey's description one guest was the same bald man in the brown Plymouth blocking her driveway. At the time, she hadn't caught the newcomer's name, or his background, but Casey was eager to share the information.

"His name is Vincent Norquay." he said. "From Vancouver, a tourist at a guess."

"Could be. At least if he's registered at your Inn, he can't be one of the thieves plaguing the village."

Casey laughed. "Is that what you thought? Why?"

"Because he spent a good five minutes blocking my driveway and staring at my building. He could have been casing the place." The last was said a bit defensively. Even to her ears the words sounded ridiculous. Plus, it had only been a couple minutes, but still.

The noise level was growing exponentially in the hallway and was not helped at all by Albert's yipping and growling.

Gladys leaned away from her phone. "Albert, settle down, boy."

Instead, the dog jumped up from his bed basket and ran to the door. The commotion in the hallway continued, and Albert began to bark again.

"What the heck is going on there?" Casey Pebbles demanded.

"I don't know, Casey. I'll have to call you back." Gladys made a note on the order sheet for the Smuggler's Inn. She kept a sheet for each customer to ensure she baked the right amount of product each week. It was a positive thing that she had to make another trip out to Whisky Corner this week.

"No, no. That's fine." Casey assured her. "I was just rambling on. You've got my order and that's all I really need. See you in a couple days," Casey said in his gravelly voice.

Gladys ended the call and sighed at Albert's barking as she tucked her phone in the back pocket of her jean walking shorts.

At least Blofeld, stretched out along the back of the couch beside her desk was undisturbed by the noise. He merely watched Albert's every move with distain in his glittering green eyes.

She got up from her tiny corner desk by the kitchen window and tugged down her flour marked red T-shirt. It didn't matter if she was untidy, the rest of the day was devoted to baking, not deliveries. Gladys crossed to the hallway door.

The arguing she initially heard turned into distinct heated words as she opened it to check out the reason for the noise.

No doubt curious too, Albert darted forward and stood in the doorway beside Gladys. He expressed his opinion by lifting his top lip and released a low snarl.

"Hush, boy."

"You stupid cow, you're responsible for this disaster. I'm going to sue you. I'll take every dime you have for this," Dwayne Davis ranted. He was dangerously red in the face and ignored Gladys to yell at Linda Leechie from 203 on the second floor. Dwayne's unit was directly under Linda's.

Gladys wondered what the stress from the argument was doing to Dwayne's angina.

The dog growled, head down, he edged forward into the hallway.

Gladys nudged him with her foot. "Stay."

Albert grumbled but plunked his butt in the doorway beside her.

Hovering by the elevator doors, Linda stood slumped shouldered, biting her lip. She was a thin woman in her late forties but looked much younger. Her limp blonde hair fell forward to cover her face. The front of her teal-blue T-shirt was wet, as was the hem of her jeans.

As if she knew she was under Gladys' scrutiny, Linda curled her bare toes into fists. Clearly, she was embarrassed and upset.

Automatically Gladys strode crossed to the younger woman and put a hand on her hunched shoulder. Albert followed closely on her heels.

"What's wrong, Linda?"

The younger woman flung up a desperate hand. "I'm so sorry, Dwayne, honestly. I don't know why these things keep happening to me." She trembled under Gladys' hand. Probably from anxiety. Dwayne's tantrums intimidated the younger woman.

The man stabbed an index finger at Linda. "I don't believe you for a second." Dwayne snarled.

His sudden movement caused Linda to jump, startled.

Gladys turned a narrow-eyed look on Dwayne. "Calm down, before you give yourself a coronary."

Dwayne growled in answer and stomped across the hallway to the condo manager's unit and pounded on the door. "Enid, get out here." His face was darkening and red travelled down the back of his neck.

He was supposedly retired from some business in Ontario, but as far as Gladys knew, no one could pin down much about Dwayne's past. He'd only been in Musgrave Landing for a few months and other than condo board meetings, Gladys had little to do with the man.

The story went he docked his boat in the marina and fell in love with the area and promptly bought into the condo complex. Before most units were sold, he took advantage of the disorganization in the early days to get himself appointed as president of the condo board. Dwayne ruled the meetings and usually would get his way with any decision. This was partly because Enid had a crush on the man and used her votes to support him, and partly because he charmed Lara Finkle who also let him run things.

At just over six feet, Dwayne's voice matched his size and attitude, deep, loud, and aggressive. He turned glittering eyes on Linda again. "I think you do these things on purpose. No one can be this stupid."

Gladys gave Linda's arm a light squeeze. "What's going on?" she asked her second floor neighbour.

Linda turned to give Gladys a bleak look, pushing hair behind her ears. "My washing machine sprung a leak and I'm flooded. By the time I got back from the grocery store, water had swamped my apartment and I think it's running down the walls to the first level. This is just like my water heater when it blew." The thin woman swallowed and ran a shaky hand over her long hair to flip the strands over her shoulder. "Dwayne said the water is running into the parking garage, under the building. I didn't know. I was concerned about his condo. Is there any water coming into yours or Matthew's place?"

"None that I noticed, at least in mine." Gladys shook her head. "I'll check Matthew's."

"Wilkes' condo isn't under your unit you stupid twit. Neither is Gladys." Dwayne tossed this over his shoulder at Linda. He turned away to hammer on the door again.

Gladys scowled at Dwayne and his name calling. "Everyone has issues from time to time, be civil."

Dwayne looked back at Gladys and lifted his lip in a sneer. "Water is pouring into the underground parking. My Cordoba is soaked, and the Corinthian leather will be ruined, not to mention the contents of my trunk." He tried to open the door of unit 101, but found it locked and threw up his hands in disgust. "I haven't even checked my condo yet. Enid needs to get someone out here to fix this mess." He turned and stabbed his finger at Linda again. "And you're paying for it. After the last time, my apartment insurance has doubled. I had to replace all the flooring in my kitchen and bathrooms. You are a disaster!"

Linda seemed to curl in on herself and Gladys patted the younger woman's shoulder.

"We remember the water heater," Gladys said with a dry tone. How could anyone forget Dwayne's whinging and whining? "It isn't like Linda blows up the plumbing on purpose." Although privately, Gladys did think water disasters seem to happen to Linda in a higher proportion then the rest of the population.

Dwayne didn't answer but beat on Enid's door once more. Like that would do any good. If she were home, Enid would have answered by now.

Linda took a shaky breath and looked over at the condo board president. "Maybe you should check your apartment, Dwayne," Linda said weakly. She then turned away from her neighbour to depress the elevator call button. Her need to leave was apparent by the way she tapped the lit button repeatedly. No doubt, to escape from the man's scathing remarks.

Linda raised one hand and covered her mouth. Eyes wide, she looked at Gladys. "Do you hear that?" Her words were slightly muffled, but clear enough.

"What?" Gladys asked with a frown.

"I think I hear running water." Her low voice didn't carry very far.

The stainless-steel doors slid open. Gladys could hear the distinct sound of running water. The faux wood-panelled back wall was moist with rivulets of water trickling down.

"Linda," she said, fairly sure of the answer before she asked. "Did you shut off the water in your unit? I mean the feed lines to the washing machine?"

Linda's navy-blue eyes locked on Gladys and widened further as she stared back. "Um, I...oh, no, I think I forgot."

"Come on," Gladys said. She tried to shoo Albert inside her unit. "Albert, you stay."

Instead, with a negative yip, the little dog zipped around her and stood in the hallway. His bouncy step and the sparkle in his dark eyes said he wasn't going to miss the fun.

The dog turned his head and spied Dwayne. He ran over to him and began barking madly, adding to the confusion.

"Get the hell away from me." Dwayne bared his teeth and raised one booted foot, as if he was prepared to kick the dog.

"Dwayne, stop it, Albert, here." Gladys called the wee dog over and then swung her condo door shut.

Dwayne emitted a wordless growl and strong armed the stairwell door. He exited stomping down the stairs to the underground parking garage.

Linda walked into the elevator.

Gladys shook her head. "We don't have time for that." They did have the world's slowest elevator. "I'm not sure it's safe to use it right now anyway. Not with water everywhere."

There was nothing to do, but to use the stairs as well. Gladys led the way to the stairwell to the left of the elevator and opened the heavy metal grey door. There was no sign of Dwayne.

"Come on. Let's go turn the water off in your apartment." She waved Linda in ahead of her. "Albert, here boy."

As she propped the fire door open, Albert scooted by. They ascended and Gladys noted the concrete steps were more than a little damp. Not a good sign if the water had made it this far.

"Oh, no." Linda's voice wobbled as dampness turned to puddles.

The three of them pounded up the stairs and exited onto the second door. As soon as they set foot on the plush gold pile carpet, water squished out from under Gladys' white runners, cool water chilled her soles. Not an altogether pleasant feeling.

They splashed their way to Linda's door and wasted a minute while she unlocked her apartment. "The laundry room is just beyond the kitchen."

Gladys brushed past the younger woman to access the utility room which housed the laundry facilities. "Yep, the same lay out as my unit," she said. "I know exactly where to find the water shut off valves for the washing machine."

They were greeted by the sound of a steady hiss of water and the smell of wildflower scented laundry detergent.

Water fountained up from behind the washing machine in a spitting flow. The floor was covered with over an inch of water. The container with the soap pods had fallen to the floor and added to the mess. Some pods were trying to make their getaway by floating out toward the kitchen.

Gladys splashed through the dull grey liquid with Albert and Linda on her heels.

"Oh." Linda's tone had added misery. She hurried over and scooped up the laundry pod container. "At least only a couple dissolved in the water." She placed the dripping container on top of the dryer.

Gladys skirted the piles of laundry on the soaked floor and avoided a pair of pink flip flops which were also floating toward the door.

Linda turned and began grabbing up the soaked clothes from the floor. She then looked around helplessly, apparently unsure where to put them. "I should have called a plumber."

"It looks like your hoses are split." The recess in the wall was where the hot and cold taps were located. There was no way to avoid getting at least a little wet. Gladys confidently reached behind the washing machine. "You should still call a plumber. At least have something done with these hoses. They need to be replaced."

"Do you even know what to do?" Linda was tossing her laundry into a blue plastic basket. Not exactly helpful, but it did keep her occupied.

Albert found a small island of bedsheets and stood on the mound to keep his feet dry while he supervised.

"My husband and I used to own a sailboat. You become very familiar with through-haul fittings and shut-off valves. This is fairly similar." She grasped a faucet handle with each hand. Both were stiff and stubbornly did not want to turn. "This is what Micky hated about gate valves." Gladys concentrated on the cold tap, using both hands.

"What?"

"This type of valve can get stuck and can fail in an emergency." Gladys said with difficulty as the wheel handle finally began to turn clockwise to close it. She moved on to the hot water and got it moving quicker. The flow of spraying water abruptly stopped.

Gladys frowned at the connections behind the washer. The metal around the connection was bent and looked damaged too. "I think, in my uneducated opinion, you might need a new washing machine."

"This is a new washing machine. I bought it just after I moved in."

Gladys shook her head as she turned to look at her neighbour. "Besides the hoses, the connections have been compromised. Maybe the machine was never hooked up properly, and finally let go all together."

"You think so? I guess it's possible. I bought the machine from that place where River Construction gave us a discount and their guy hooked it up for me."

"Still, that shouldn't have caused a water leak, especially this bad." Gladys opened the washer and looked inside. The tub was wet, and so was the clothing inside. However, the water level was low, only a few inches from the bottom.

Sucking air in between her teeth, Gladys braced two hands on the front of the washer and tipped the machine back. Water cascaded out from under the machine with flecks of rust. "I'd say there's your next problem. The tub has at least one hole too."

"But it's brand new," Linda shook her head. "How could this happen?" She grabbed up the half-soaked sheets from the floor, dislodging Albert from his dry perch.

"There's time to worry about it later. For now, grab the bucket and start dumping the water down the laundry sink drain. I'll use your mop." She extracted the mop and used her left foot to push the bucket toward Linda to begin the cleanup.

"What? Oh, okay." Linda put down the bundle of dripping sheets on top of the washer. She picked up the red plastic bucket and scooped up a quarter pail of water, and then looked around uncertainly again.

Gladys pursed her lips at the other woman. "The laundry sink, Linda. Toss the water out there." Gladys flipped the water-soaked mop around and wrung the fabric head out over the heavy-duty white plastic sink. She moved to the right side to make room for Linda.

"Yes, yes, right. I'm sorry."

"You're just a bit overwhelmed. Don't worry about it. There are no dead bodies at the end of this. All of it can be fixed."

Albert danced back out of the deeper water and watched the women work from the doorway. As she mopped the floor, Gladys saw the dog alternately lifting one wet foot at a time to stand on only three. She snorted a laugh, shaking her head at the dog.

They worked in silence for several minutes clearing the water from the laundry room floor. Linda moved to the sodden carpet, using bath towels to absorb the water. Gladys worked the mop along the base boards outside the utility room.

Albert scooted over to Gladys and stood on a damp section behind her.

Linda deposited the wet towels in a moist pile on the utility room floor. "So, why do you have Albert?" She asked as she grabbed a large sponge from an overhead cupboard and went to work on the water soaking the carpet to the hallway.

She used the sponge to absorb as much water as it could hold before squeezing it out into the bucket. "Where is Mathew anyway?"

Gladys continued to mop the floor but lifted her eyebrows at the other woman. She wondered what Linda really wanted to know. "He's in Spain, Barcelona, actually."

"Working?"

"Yes, he'll be back at the end of the week, Sunday I think."

"Oh, good." Linda squeezed the sponge out over the bucket. She didn't meet Gladys's eyes, and her cheeks were flushed. "We don't have to mention this incident to Matthew, do we?"

Gladys's lips curved into a half smile. "That depends on whether Matthew's place took any damage. I suspect not, but I'll check. Regardless, it's not my story to tell, but you know it will come out sometime. Probably at the next condo board meeting."

"Yes, true." There was misery in Linda's tone. She squeezed her eyes shut briefly, then flipped her hair back over her shoulder, and continued with the job.

Gladys felt sorry for Linda's embarrassment. She must have some feelings for Matthew and didn't want to look bad in his eyes.

The pair worked for several more minutes and did a fair job of clearing up the water Gladys judged.

"The carpets are going to require a steam cleaner," Linda commented.

Albert barked once and ran to the door.

"What is that dog doing out of Matthew Wilkes' apartment?" A stern voice flowed to them from the apartment hallway over Albert's barking.

Both Linda and Gladys swivelled their heads as the newcomer came into view. Albert was doing his best to raise the alarm. Apparently, Dwayne had found the building manager. For his part, the dog continued to bark sharply at Enid, who had just walked right in.

"Albert," Gladys said sharply. "Enough, come here."

Enid Lindquist squinted over her heavy black frame glasses and down her nose at Albert with obvious distaste. "According to the condo board bylaws, animals are not allowed to wander the hallways of this building."

"He's fine." Linda said firmly to Enid. "This is my apartment, and Albert's more than welcome here."

Albert lifted his top lip at the manager as he backed up. The dog emitted one more growl at the large, stern woman before scooting over to stand behind Gladys. She shushed the dog, and while he stopped barking, he continued to watch Enid. Gladys thought Albert was a good judge of character. She didn't care for Enid either.

The building manager was several inches taller than Gladys's five-foot-three inches. She carried her bulk like she was a prize fighter. By the lack of shades or highlights in her hair, it was obvious the jet-black colour came from a bottle. Her pitch-black hair was pulled back into a severe style on the back of her head. This, combined with eyebrows plucked to a thin line, and glittering dark eyes, gave the building manger a forbidding expression. As an elementary teacher, before she changed jobs, Enid must have been a terror in the school system.

Today, Enid wore a long, burgundy-coloured skirt with a light pink cotton blouse. The colours alternated, but the clothing style was the same each day, like a uniform. Gladys figured somewhere in Enid's past she must have worked as a prison guard before getting into education.

Albert emitted another low growl and Gladys hushed him. "There was an emergency. We needed to shut off Linda's water," she said to the building manager.

"Another flood, yes, Dwayne told me." Enid turned her glare on Linda. "If you'd paid for the appliances the builder recommended, you wouldn't have these problems, but no, you had to buy the cheap second-hand crap." She shifted her accusatory gaze to survey the room. "First the hot water heater, then the dishwasher, now this."

"I didn't, I bought–"

But Enid cut off Linda's words. "You're going to pay for the damage." Enid turned a flat stare on Linda, and the other woman cringed, biting her bottom lip. "This is the limit. You are a one-person tsunami."

"I have insurance," Linda stated in a quivering voice. She might have been trying to sound defiant but failed.

Enid's lips tightened as she narrowed her gaze at Linda. "You'd better," she said menacingly.

Gladys frowned at Enid. "Linda, maybe you should give your insurance agent a call right now?" The dog let out one more bark. She realized Albert wasn't going to settle down anytime soon. She straightened from leaning over the laundry sink and wringing out the mop. "It's probably time for me and

Albert to go." She wiped her wet hands on the thighs of her denim shorts.

"Thank you for all your help, Gladys." Linda gave her neighbour a weak smile.

"No problem, it's what neighbours do." Gladys edged her way toward the door. "Come on, Albert." It was time to fade to the background. The terrier scurried after her.

Chapter Seven

Gladys exited the stairs back onto the first floor. She was in time to see Dwayne brace his hands on either side of the opening and lean into the elevator car. She raised her eyebrows puzzled and would have walked right over to investigate, but Albert began his growling and barking routine.

"What has gotten into you? Come on." Gladys crossed to her unit and unlocked the door for the dog. For a moment she was worried he wouldn't budge, but Albert scooted inside without any urging. She closed the door and crossed the open space to the elevator. "What are you looking at? You shouldn't use the elevator—"

"Shh," Dwayne said sharply.

She raised her eyebrows at this, then she heard it. A buzzing sound, like water dripped on a hot burner. "Oh, my." Gladys stepped well back from the elevator and covered her mouth with the fingers of her left hand. "This is not good."

"Somewhere water must be getting into the electrical connections." Dwayne looked up at the ceiling panels inside the elevator as if he could see the problem.

Like a gentle waterfall, moisture continued to run in thin rivulets down the walls inside the elevator. "I shut off Linda's water. This has to stop soon."

Dwayne grunted. "Might be too late."

"Should we shut off the electrical breakers for the elevator? The flooding may have made it unsafe. Everyone will have to use the stairs."

He sniffed and turned to look at her. "Knock yourself out." Dwayne's tone was terse, and his eyes had the squinty angry look he'd get at condo board meetings when he wasn't getting his way.

"Did you check your condo? How is your unit fairing?"

"It's wet," he snapped. Dwayne stalked toward the stairwell door. He almost knocked into Freddie who was entering the front foyer carrying a large duffle bag.

"Whoa, there dude," the newest arrival exclaimed. The glare Dwayne shot his way made the other man raise his hands in self-defence.

Dwayne ignored Freddie and exited. The sound of his cowboy boots reverberated back to them as he stomped down the stairs, no doubt headed to the lower parking level.

Freddie and Gladys glanced at each other. They could hear him curse 'Leaky Linda' and other uncharitable remarks about water in general all the way down the stairs until the basement door closed behind him.

"What is going on?" Freddie asked, blinking.

"We have a bit of a calamity on our hands again, I'm afraid." Gladys sighed and gestured inside of the elevator car.

The lanky man let the shoulder strap on his duffle drop off his shoulder before leaning in to look at the interior.

"No," he said, disbelievingly. "Not Linda, not again?" Freddie rolled his dark-brown eyes and eased his olive-green duffle bag to the floor Which was covered with wet footprints.

"I'm afraid so." Gladys gave Freddie a telling look.

"Not her dishwasher connection again?" Freddie shook his head and allowed a partial smile; yellowed teeth were exposed.

"No, her washing machine hoses sprung a leak. It flooded her apartment and some of the hallway this time. And some in Dwayne's unit again."

"And the elevator."

Gladys nodded. "And the elevator. Oh, and to hear Dwayne tell it, the water has entered into the parking garage below. Probably through the elevator shaft."

"That wouldn't surprise me." Freddie gestured at the sodden elevator. "Looks like the worst of it has stopped though." He glanced at the door of unit 103, Dwayne Davis' apartment. "And Dwayne's condo took damage again?"

"Some, I think. He was more concerned about his car."

Freddie grunted and picked up his duffle bag. "I'm not looking forward this next special assessment notice."

"Me, neither. I'm going to find Norm. The elevator isn't safe." She'd rather speak with her old friend than deal with Enid.

Gladys strode past Freddie and left out the back door. There was a garden shed on the back of the property she'd try first, but this wasn't necessary as she spotted his red and blue cap just beyond the white roses to the left of the parking lot. She waved at the man and called his name to get his attention.

He met her halfway.

"Do you know where or how to shut off the breakers to the elevator? I think it's become unsafe," Gladys said as she reached him. Quickly, she outlined the situation.

"That woman has the worst luck." Norm propped his garden weeding claw against a tree. "Yep, I know how to decommission the elevator." He turned and walked back to the building. Gladys walked with him but had to hurry to keep up with his longer strides.

Gladys shook her head. "Linda took the contractor's recommendations on her appliances and River Construction installed them for her." She pursed her lips as she thought about this.

Norm shrugged his thin shoulders. "Who knows?" He pulled on the metal retractable key chain on his belt and unlocked the door beside the giant metal garage door. He glanced up at Gladys, as he hesitated.

"What is it, Norm?"

"Just gossip I've heard, but the condo board might want to look into who did the plumbing and electrical inspections is all."

"Wouldn't that have been a provincial inspector requested by the municipality?"

"Maybe, I'm not all together certain. Like I said, it's gossip, but–" he cut off his words with a shrug and opened the man door which led to the basement parking area. "You might want to tell Enid to put up a sign up or something, to let people know the elevator is out of commission."

"Will do, thanks."

Gladys returned to the foyer and found Freddie standing guard in front of the elevator. She didn't want to spread gossip, but as a resident, Freddie had a right to know what Norm had said, so she shared it. "I think this building was put up with substandard materials to go along with the poor workmanship. I'm going to push for a new plumber to be brought in. Someone other than who Enid wants, for an independent opinion."

"That's not a bad idea, but can you do that? I think that's something to do with the builder's warranty, isn't it?"

She lifted her eyebrows at Freddie. "Randy River declared bankruptcy mere days after the building was signed off by Pink Brick. Matthew couldn't find out where the builder went. His office in Ganges is empty."

"Don't bad builders usually just changes their business name and start again?"

"I suppose so, but we couldn't find a new contract business under his name anywhere either. Anyway, River Construction doesn't get a say, not anymore. I doubt there is any warranty."

"What's bugging me is I took the builder's recommendation too. Maybe I should check my appliances for problems." Freddie picked up his bag and flipped the strap of his duffle over his shoulder.

The front entrance door abruptly swung open. The glass and steel frame would have hit the wall with the force of Lara Finkle's shove if it were not for the restraining arm.

Her face was flushed and hair askew. "What?" She snapped at Gladys.

"Nothing," Gladys shook her head, shocked at Lara tone. She folded her hands over her middle as she watched the other woman stalk past her, bound for the elevator.

Gladys opened her mouth to tell Lara not to use the elevator when Lara spied Freddie and rocked to a stop. Her jaw tightened as her eyes narrowed. Freddie took a tentative step back.

"You." Lara stabbed an index finger at him. Her red-lacquered fingernail looked like a talon. "Those cannabis plants of yours stink to high heaven. They make the whole building reek. Get rid of them or we'll get rid of you."

Gladys took a couple steps back herself. This wasn't her business, and she didn't want to referee an argument.

Freddie's wiry hair looked as chaotic as Lara's, as he ran an agitated hand through the frizz. Still, he drew himself up, straightening his back and lost his customary slouch. "No, I don't think so."

Gladys slipped her hand into her right front pocket for her door key as she watched the two.

Lara narrowed her eyes at him and turned up the intensity. "Get rid of that marijuana grow op you've got going or I'll have it done for you."

Unabashed, Gladys listened in as she unlocked the door.

Her second-floor neighbour lifted his chin. "You and who's army? I'm allowed five plants for medicinal use, by law. There's nothing you can do about it."

"Oh yeah, we'll see about that. I have allergies. Your right to smoke up doesn't override my right to breathe clean air. The cops are coming here within the hour. I'm going to tell them about your grow op."

"Go ahead." Freddie shrugged. "I have a condition that must be treated." He sounded confidently defiant and yet edged further away from Lara, toward the stairs. "I have my cert card and the paperwork is all in order from the Ministry of Health."

"I bet," Lara snapped. She turned away to step into the elevator.

The sound of someone plodding down the steps in the stairwell filled the awkward silence. Enid brushed past Freddie.

"Lara," Enid strode over to Lara Finkle. "You can't use the elevator it might not be safe," she said. "I haven't posted a sign yet, but I will."

Lara expelled air through her nose, "Now what?" She looked at Enid and flung up her hands. "Why is the elevator out? What's going on?"

Enid pointed upward to the second floor. "Leaky Linda, that's what. She caused another flood. It's her low-end, crappy appliances at fault." Enid turned to look at Gladys. "It's her fault." She tipped her head as she addressed Gladys. "Gladys wanted each condo owner to have the freedom to choose their own appliances along with the other finishes. You all voted for that. This is what I get for allowing you lot to make the rules."

It was true Gladys had been the one to table the motion to allow the choice. That way she could bring her own things, if she chose, instead of buying new ones through the builder.

She straightened her spine and lifted her chin, just as Freddie had and marched over to the pair. "If you remember, Dwayne voted in favour of that choice along with me, Linda, and Matthew. You might be the building manager, Enid, but you don't make the rules. You may have two votes, but the majority rules. And the majority of unit owners decide what we can, and cannot do, in our own building. Don't overstep your authority, someone else can be chosen as building manager. All

it takes is a simple tabled motion and a vote. Remember that."
Gladys gave the taller woman an emphatic nod.

She then turned on one heel and stalked away from the
pair of disagreeable women. With one hand on her unit's door
lever, she realized one other thing needed to be said. So, Gladys
turned back and met Enid's glare. "For your information, Linda
did take the builders recommendations, why do you think her
insurance company backed her up the last two times?"

Enid narrowed her eyes at Gladys but said nothing. It was
at that moment the power to the elevator was cut, and the
lights inside and out of conveyance went out. Norm had shut
off the breakers.

Gladys left Lara and Enid standing in the hallway as
Freddie backed away and entered the stairwell, making good
his escape.

Chapter Eight

Gladys made a cup of strong black tea and took it outside to the patio. She flopped down on her wicker love seat in the shade. The quiet rustling of birds in a nearby tree, some calling out to others, was the only excitement. Even these sounds were not intrusive but blended well with the setting. She needed a bit of peace to calm down. Watching the waters of the Narrows sparkle and shift beyond the marina as the tide ebbed helped.

Her home was quiet, and the patio was a welcome oasis of calm. Back in the utility room, Albert began snoring in his basket bed. She chuckled at the sound and sipped her tea.

The sun warmed the reddish-pink patio brick. With the toe of her right foot, Gladys pulled over a wicker ottoman. She toed off her damp running shoes and put her feet up. Sighing happily as the sun now shone on her pink feet, warming them too.

Confrontations were never a nice thing as far as Gladys was concerned. She hated them. It was less stressful to send a stern email or write a carefully thought-out report. However, sometimes those actions were not enough, and she had to say something. Trouble was, having spoken her mind, Gladys now felt badly. She rehashed the whole incident over and over in her mind, looking for a better way to have dealt with the adversity. What she could have said differently or something. Her minded churned away in circles, reliving the skirmish with Enid. Always a fruitless endeavour. She breathed in deeply and exhaled slowly in an attempt to calm her mood.

Blofeld took this opportunity to slink down from the top of his cat post and ooze up onto the love seat beside Gladys. He squirmed, and his head popped up under Gladys' forearm.

"Hello, my love." She rubbed the cat behind his ears.

His massive fluffy paws settled on her thigh in a bid for more attention. Stroking the large white Persian helped sooth her ruffled nerves further. Especially when the cat began to purr and knead her chunky leg. Good thing she was wearing denim.

Blofeld's company was soothing, and Gladys relaxed as she sipped her tea. Eventually she came to conclusion she'd said nothing wrong. Enid was a bully, like Dwayne, and if left unchecked, would try and run roughshod over all the residents. It wasn't a job she wanted, but someone had to stick up for Linda.

Half an hour later, Gladys heard Maisy return. She must have dozed off in her sunspot, the sound of the door opening brought her awake and blinking.

Now that they were no longer alone, Blofeld, as per usual, slunk back to his post. He was an old cat, at fourteen, and not inclined to spare any notice of others. He ignored everyone who was not Gladys from his perch in the living room.

Gladys climbed to her feet and put her now dry shoes back on. She then followed the cat inside. "Well, my girl?" Gladys asked her granddaughter, as she stopped in the kitchen to put her mug in the sink.

Maisy had paused to scratch Albert behind his ears after she came in the door. The dog gave one yip in hello, but otherwise stayed curled up in the basket by the utility room door.

The girl straightened and she grinned from ear-to-ear. "I got the job," she said, and a laugh bubbled out. Sweetly, she gave a little shrug and her cheeks flush to pink.

Gladys couldn't help but smile along with her granddaughter's joy. "Good for you, I knew you would." She washed her hands and then picked up a golden baked loaf, cooled but still in the pan. "What are your hours?" She picked up a butter knife and ran it around the edge of the metal pan. The bread was popped onto the rack on the back of the counter, beside the big mixer.

"I only work four hours a day, five days a week, but it's a start." Maisy joined her grandmother in the kitchen, and she washed her hands too.

The young girl's excitement was affecting Gladys, causing her mood to lift. "A very good start it is," she said with a smile, moving on to a third loaf pan.

"If things pick up like last summer, Jane said I could be working more."

"Even better. When do you go in?" She dealt with the last loaf.

"Today to start my training. Right after lunch. So, I'd like to ask you for another favour." Maisy nibbled her bottom lip as she began gathering up the loaf pans and stacked them in the double sink.

"Absolutely." Gladys stuck the plug in the sink, turned on the hot water, and squirted in soap.

"I'll walk Albert before I go work and then I'll put him in Matthew's apartment. Could you please let him outside around three o'clock, if I'm not back by then?"

Gladys was pleased by the hesitance in Maisy's tone. The girl didn't take it for granted her grandmother would accommodate her new job. "I certainly can. I'll keep him here with me after he's had a tinkle. This is my last batch of bread for the Farmer's Market. So, it's no problem."

"Thank you! I'll scrub these pans for you." Maisy said in a rush words.

Gladys nodded. "That would be a great help, thanks." She handed her granddaughter an apron. "I'll make us something to eat."

Maisy nodded and donned the apron then set to work washing the bread pans.

On an adjacent counter, Gladys began gathering items to assemble chicken salad for sandwiches with sunrise coleslaw.

"When I got home, there was a cop car parked in the lot. I directed a police officer to Lara Finkle's unit." Maisy looked over her shoulder at her grandmother. "Do you know what that could be about? You don't get many RCMP here in the village, do you?

"No, we don't. That reminds me, you can't use the elevator until it's been inspected. There's been a water leak on the second floor. The elevator has been powered off until then. I'm sure it's nothing serious, but better to be safe."

Maisy nodded. "I saw the out-of-order sign on the elevator panel. That's why I showed Constable Tadmore where the stairs were."

"Oh. Norm must have spoken to Enid. I forgot to tell her to put up a sign."

Maisy's eyes darted away, and she became very interested in rinsing each pan with hot water cascading into the double sink before stacking the bread pans carefully on the rack.

Gladys tipped her head to one side as she studied Maisy's blush. She bit back a smile. "Tall, dark, and handsome, was the officer?"

She grabbed the pot scrubber from the ceramic frog by the taps. "Yes, he is." She said a bit breathlessly. "Constable Tadmore has to be at least six and half feet tall. I don't run into too many guys taller than me."

"Mm," Gladys said and sliced a couple of green onions length-ways before dicing them. "He didn't say anything about a theft, did he?"

Now Maisy did look up at her grandmother. "No? What happened?"

"I heard Lara Finkle was robbed last night." She scrapped the onion in with the chopped chicken breast, mayonnaise, parsley, and pepper. No salt for her, not with her blood pressure. "She was expecting the RCMP to drop by sometime today. Constable Tadmore must be here for that incident." She used a fork to stir the salad ingredients into the dressing.

"Was Ms. Finkle at home at the time? Do you know what was stolen?" Maisy finished with another pan, rinsed it, and put it on the rack to drain.

Gladys put the chicken salad and coleslaw on the table and added a basket of fresh rolls along with plates and silverware. "I don't know, but I'm betting the thief made off with something quite valuable. She was very upset according to Arlie Birch when she was in the café this morning." She picked up a yellow cotton tea towel and began drying the bread pans.

"I don't understand how someone could get in. The entrance doors are locked after seven o'clock. You'd need a key."

"I know." Gladys picked up another pan, dried it, and stacked it inside the first. She'd put them in the top oven to air dry properly after their meal.

"Maybe it was an inside job," Maisy said, but her remark was off the cuff. Her attention was on scrubbing the cooked butter off the side of a loaf pan.

"I doubt that." Gladys' response was merely reflex. She knew her neighbours, they'd were all honest people. She paused, weren't they?

A disturbing thought made her slowly turn to look at Albert as she automatically wiped soap suds from the bread pan. The wee dog was deep asleep, and gently snoring.

No, Albert's condition was the result of an accident. Her gaze shifted to Maisy. She was not going to bring it up, but her granddaughter was an intelligent girl and perceptive.

Maisy lifted her head and looked at her grandmother. "You don't think the same thief broke into Matthew's place, stole his cappuccino maker, and pushed Albert off the balcony, do you?" Then her eyebrows crept up to her hairline. "That's why Matthew wanted a dog sitter and a house sitter."

Gladys shook her head. "He never mentioned anything about being robbed. What's this about his cappuccino machine?"

"He mentioned it when I went over to get his keys." Maisy pulled the plug on the sink. "Matthew doesn't have much in his apartment. So, he was very annoyed with the loss of the coffee maker."

"I know, that's why I insisted you come here to eat. I don't know what you'd cook with over there if you wanted to."

"He's got a microwave." Maisy said doubtfully. "I'd rather eat your cooking than mine anyway."

"Still, if these break-ins are happening at night. I think you should sleep here in the guest room from now on. Albert can stay here too, until Matthew gets back."

Maisy looked at her grandmother for a moment. She nibbled her bottom lip as she thought, then she shook her head, making her baby-fine blonde curls bounce against her golden cheeks. "I'm fine, Grandma. The thief already hit Matthew's place so they know Matthew has nothing worth stealing. The guy barely has anything beyond a bed and an ancient floor model TV. Plus, I keep the doors locked and you are just across the hallway."

"Maisy, I really think–"

"I'm good, Grandma, really. I doubt the thief will be back. Besides, Albert is a good security alarm. We have zero pigeons on the balcony in the morning." She gave her grandmother a half smile. "Anyway, I'm back here Sunday. I want to honestly earn the money Matthew paid me to look after his place."

Gladys frowned but let the issue go, for now.

THAT EVENING, THE NEW moon was slowing beginning to rise at half ten when Arlie and Gladys drove to the new pump house. And a good thing the usually gibbous orb was merely a small sliver of its former self. Else, someone might see the pair of them, or worse, what they were doing and report them.

Earlier during dinner, Linda had dropped by to thank Gladys for her help mopping up the flood.

"Did you get a plumber to come out?" Gladys waved Linda into a seat and placed a slice of blackberry pie in front of her.

"First, I tried those guys across the street, Heith's Plumbing, but when I called the number, they said they only handle industrial sized jobs. So, I tried Frank's Plumbing, he came right out." Linda accepted the bowl of whipping cream Maisy handed her and plopped a dollop on her pie. "Frank is not impressed with the plumbing job in my apartment. He says it's crap, pure and simple. He's going to change the washer hoses and redo all my plumbing connections."

"That will be pricey." Gladys poured tea for their guest.

"I know, but better that than another flood. I think Dwayne was ready to murder me." She gave a weak laugh.

"Did you need to finish your laundry? You can use my machines." Gladys sat down across from Linda.

In the end, Maisy had offered to wash Linda's clothes for her that evening while Linda ran the carpet cleaner, she'd rented over all the affected areas. At least Maisy wouldn't be alone while she was out. Gladys was still unsettled about the idea of a thief somehow getting access to her building. She wished Matthew had mentioned his missing cappuccino maker. She would not have encouraged Maisy to house sit for her neighbour if she'd known.

Arlie parked his truck in the deep shadows behind the pump house. The bulk of the new black granite building hid the half ton from any traffic on the Whisky Creek Road.

They got out and as quietly as they could, hauled the ladder out of the back of his truck.

The industrial yard light cast even more shadows on the sides of the compact building. The weak orange glow was no doubt the reason Arlie stumbled and dropped his end of the aluminum extension ladder. Gladys gasped at the noise and rocked to a halt.

"Oh, for heaven's sake." He snatched the ladder off the ground impatiently, likely annoyed at himself for dropping it.

"Shh." Gladys glanced toward the closest house some fifty feet away. The white paper she held bounced out with the jolt of Arlie's actions. "Darn it." She grabbed the batch of paper and tried to get it out of sight. Unfortunately, even folded, the banner was too large for her windbreaker pockets.

The pair paused, and shared a wide-eyed, yet excited glance. The white paper glowed like a beacon. They were wearing dark jackets, jeans, and baseball caps. The clothing should help conceal their presence. Each held still and waited to see if they'd been heard. When no one from the closest houses raised the alarm, she gestured to Arlie, and they moved forward.

Arlie snickered as Gladys tried to shield the banner from casual view with her arm over it. "Once we begin to hang the banner, there would be little you can do to conceal it."

"Hopefully we'll be quick and can make a fast getaway. I want to be long gone before anyone notices the new sign hung over the pump house door."

Gladys' heart thumped in her chest as she followed her partner in crime. "I'm sure no one can see us in this dim light," Gladys whispered. The rush of adrenaline was one of the reasons she helped Arlie with this crazy serial prank. She felt adventurous, and a touch reckless. Like a naughty teenager out after curfew.

"It's surprising they didn't spring for better quality lighting, like LED bulbs." Arlie grunted in disgust as they negotiated the aluminium ladder around the corner of the building.

"I'm betting this lighting was the only cost saving measure."

"I wonder if someone in the municipality had a vested interest in the materials supplied to build this place." Arlie tone was low.

"Meaning what?" She kept her voice soft, just above a whisper.

Arlie set the ladder's feet on the pavement and leaned it against the black granite facade. "Maybe one of them has part ownership in a business that supplied the granite, or the cedar, or something."

Gladys gave a head waggle. "Could be." True, she wasn't happy with the final cost of the new facility either. She'd been as shocked as the rest of the Musgrave Landing Seniors' Group. They'd heard the news at one Sunday coffee after church. Councillor Nickle had let the full cost slip. Well, actually Arlie had wormed it out of her, and it didn't take long for the news to get around.

Earl Moffatt had suggested some kind of protest in front of the village office. Possibly signs and what not, but the plan was vague, and his suggestion soon fizzled.

Gladys offered the banner idea to Arlie as they drove home that Sunday. "It's a way of expressing our dissatisfaction with the levels of government and their wasteful spending."

"I don't know how much good something like that would do, but it would be funny." Arlie rubbed his chin as he thought about it. He glanced her way as they sat at a stop sign and waited for traffic to pass. "What gave you the idea?"

She winked at him. "You did, with your jokes about how the building could be mistaken for a restaurant or café. You inspired me."

Arlie lifted salt and pepper eyebrows. "Jokes? I suppose they were. I thought I was being sarcastic."

"Besides, we need something peaceful, and to the point. Protesting or picketing might be difficult for some of us. Not everyone is able-bodied."

"True." He released the brake and they continued down High Street. "Plus, it's nearly impossible to get any kind of agreement out of that group anyway. Everyone is appalled, but not prepared to actually do anything about the situation." Arlie had agreed.

"If it's just you and I, we can keep it secret."

Arlie had nodded. "I like that, keep them guessing who is putting up the signs. It'll give me a reason to use my old pen plotter too."

"What's a pen plotter?"

"A very large printer. We will need a very large banner." He'd winked back at her.

Once the first banner was in place, Gladys had taken photos. When she got home, she'd sent the pictures to the community paper, the Village Voice, via a pseudonym Facebook account.

Ida and Jessie, the Fisher twins, co-editors of the Voice investigated and published a piece in the paper the same week. The villagers of Musgrave Landing were happy to send photo links to their Member of the Legislative Assembly in support of the protest. Cutting and pasting a link and then sharing it, was easier than marching and picketing.

So far, sending emails to the bigger news organizations hadn't garnered any attention and maybe it never would, but one had to make an effort.

Tonight, she'd brought her own phone to take pictures. When she got home, she'd send another message to the Village Voice. She wanted Ida to get the photos in next weeks' issue. They hadn't planned on doing a lot of banners, but Ann spoiled the fun by tearing down the first. Then too, Arlie was having a grand time coming up with new slogans. She could see these nighttime shenanigans might go on for a while, and that was okay. These escapades got her mind off the condo board, and her growing financial stress.

Gladys wondered if any of the other unit owners had money issues with the extra payments. Maybe some did, but others probably did not.

They reached the north end of the building with the fancy cedar beam entrance facing the road. Arlie grasped the sides of the ladder and extended the device an extra five feet.

The clunking of the locking mechanism sounded too loud in the still evening. It made a thunk and clunk noise that seemed to carry miles. They glanced at each other, a bit wide-eyed.

Gladys shifted impatiently from foot to foot. "If we aren't spotted tonight, it will be a miracle."

Arlie grunted as he put the toes of each foot against the corresponding foot of the ladder. He then raised his arms parallel to the ground. He'd performed this same maneuver the first time and now she had to ask.

"What are you doing?"

"Making sure the ladder is at the proper angle." He adjusted the ladder's feet two inches. "OHSA regs."

"What? Oh, I get you, Occupational Health and Safety." She nodded.

Arlie grasped the rungs and opened the ladder a few feet taller. He began to fiddle with something.

"Now what are you doing?" she hissed at Arlie.

"One of the clips won't reposition to lock the ladder in place. Give me a minute."

She pulled the cylinder of paper free of her coat and smoothed it flat against her middle.

"I've been thinking, maybe I should put up a poll on the community page this time to gather in the rest of the villagers. I'm sure they'd like to express their opinion too. Then our MLA will see how annoyed voters are."

"Not a bad idea."

"The community page has built-in survey functionality. The impact would be more legitimate with resident's names attached to the result. I can suggest it to Ida, and then the paper could run the poll in both the print and digital issues."

Arlie fiddled with something on the underside of the ladder. "Won't Ida figure out you are part of the banner protest then?"

"Maybe, but everyone wants to know who made the spending decisions on this place, and how much our taxes are going to go up because of it." The last thing Gladys could afford right now was higher taxes.

"That's a fact. There was lots of talk about it today in the café. Momentum is growing."

"Speaking of the café, how did Maisy make out?"

Arlie finished positioning the ladder under the eaves trough to his satisfaction and finally got the clip to lock. "She's going to be just fine. Maisy is a quick learner and has a good personality for working with the public. I think we got a few more young people stopping by merely because I got her to serve a table on the patio when it got busy."

"Oh, good." Gladys had been sure her granddaughter would do just fine, but it was a relief to have her faith confirmed.

He adjusted the bottom feet one more time and then turned to look at Gladys. "Up you go." Arlie waved at the ladder.

"I put the banner up the first time. It's your turn." She thrust the bundle of paper and zip ties at him, but he didn't move to take it. "I'll hold the ladder for you."

"Oh for—" he grumbled. "Fine." He scaled the ladder. If it was possible for him to stomp his feet as he climbed, Arlie did just that. Gladys hurried forward to brace the vibrating length of aluminum and hopefully reduce the noise.

Arlie reached the level where he could attach the banner end to the eaves bracket and stuck out his hand. "Zip tie, please."

Gladys handed up one tie and offered one end of the banner. "Here you go."

Arlie looped the plastic through the hole he'd already punched in the paper after he'd finished printing the banner. "I'm kinda proud of this one."

"Are you?"

A car engine revved as it came down the road.

"Get down, they'll see us." Gladys hissed.

He dropped banner and hurriedly, Arlie pounded down the ladder and made to grab it.

"Just leave it, come on."

They scurried behind the building.

Gladys peeked around the corner and narrowed her eyes. A late model car slowed as it drove by. As it passed the house across the street, she could see by the yard light it was a brown Plymouth. The vehicle crawled slowly past the pump house.

"He's going so slow, he has to see the ladder." She covered her mouth with her left hand. One end of the banner hung from the eaves trough and appeared to glow in the dim light.

As the Plymouth passed by the building, the car sped up again. The driver was on his way to Whisky Corner, and apparently wasn't curious enough about what was going on to stop.

She frowned. Why would a tourist from Vancouver be scoping out the pump house at ten o'clock at night? Or was she imaging his interest?

Once the engine noise faded, Arlie heaved a sigh of relief.

Gladys shifted her gaze to her friend and took in his stressed expression. "You were afraid it was Ann Westcott." Gladys grinned at him

"You got that right. Our mayor can be scary."

"True."

"Did you recognize that car or the driver?" Arlie led the way back to the ladder.

"He was hanging out by my place earlier today."

"A visitor?"

"A tourist, at least Casey Pebbles says so. His name is Vinny Norquay and he's staying at The Smuggler's Inn."

Arlie grunted. "Trust Casey to know." He scaled the ladder to finish the job.

Chapter Nine

The next morning, Gladys was in her kitchen again. It was early yet, even though the sun was well up. A raspberry tear and share had just gone into the bottom oven. She wanted it to still be warm when Maisy came across the hall for breakfast.

Thinking of her granddaughter seemed to make the girl appear. Maisy tapped on the door and then stepped inside, closely followed by Albert. "Morning, Grandma."

Gladys' lips twitched in amusement as the dog once again raced to Blofeld's dishes and checked out what the cat had for breakfast. Blofeld had eaten earlier when she did. Now the bowl contained a handful of puppy chow and apparently, it tasted just fine to Albert. "Good morning, dear. How did you sleep?" She got out another coffee mug out of the upper cupboard above the coffee maker.

"Great, it's so quiet compared to Vancouver. I can breathe here, I'm loving it."

Gladys's smile spread wider. "I like the sound of that. Are you ready for your first day of paid work?" She rested one hip against the granite countertop edge.

"I'm a bit nervous about it. I wanted to talk to you about that." Maisy slid onto one of the dark wooden peninsula stools. "I could work, they want me to, but I agreed to help you at the farmer's market at the marina. I don't want to leave you high and dry. Jane said to speak to you and then decide."

Gladys poured a mug of coffee for Maisy and passed it to girl. "What do you want to do?" She pushed a high kitchen stool toward her granddaughter for her to take a seat.

"I want to do both." Maisy sat and folded her hands around the mug and then took a sip.

"That's not possible, my girl." She sipped from her own mug.

"I know, I'll tell Jane I can't work Wednesdays."

"You will do no such thing." Gladys folded her arms and yet still held her coffee cup in her right hand. She had lots of practice with this maneuver.

"But how can I–"

Her grandmother shook her head. "This is your first paying job for someone other than family. You can use Jane as a reference for the next job you want to try for. That is a real and tangible asset."

Maisy bit her lip as she mulled this over. "But I agreed to help you with your business before I even came to Salt Spring Island. I feel like I'm letting you down."

"Don't worry, you're not. The fact you're concerned about it, does you credit. I'm quite fine with you shifting over to this new job. The experience will be good for you. Plus, you'll make more in tips."

The oven timer sounded at the same time as the phone rang.

"Can you take out the tear and share, please, while I get this?" Gladys quickly wiped her hands.

"Sure." Maisy hopped up from the stool and grabbed the oven mitts from the counter.

Gladys dug her cell phone out of the back pocket of her red cotton shorts. She put the old-style flip phone to her ear as she tugged down her pink T-shirt.

"Grandma," Maisy said, and Gladys moved out of the way of the oven door.

"Hello?"

"I know it's you!" The words were shouted, and Gladys had to move the phone away from her ear.

She glanced at her granddaughter. It was plain Maisy had no problem hearing the agitated woman at the other end of the call

"I know you're doing it. It's you and Arlie Birch, isn't it? He says it's not him, but I know otherwise. This isn't funny, you know!"

"What's not funny, Ann?" Gladys played for time.

"Don't play stupid with me. 'Coming soon, Chicken and Rib Extravaganza,'" Ann's voice was a high-pitched squeak. No doubt from stress. "I had Zeke tear down that stupid chicken restaurant sign. Just stop it or I'll call the police on you." Abruptly the intense words stopped as the conversation was ended by the caller.

Maisy stared at her grandmother, holding the baking pan with the golden-brown breakfast treat. "What the heck was that about?"

Her grandmother gestured to the cooling rack and Maisy placed the pan on it. "Oh, that was just our mayor, Ann

Westcott. She was having a tiny melt down." Gladys tucked her phone away into her back pocket. She washed her hands and extracted the bread to place on a serving plate. The scent of raspberry and fresh bread filled the air as the creation gently steamed.

Gladys picked up the carafe of coffee and gestured to Maisy.

"Yes, please."

She poured more coffee. "Apparently, someone has taken exception to the elaborate pump house the municipality built to back up our water supply."

"Who would have a problem with the new pump house?" Maisy sat down and sipped the coffee.

"No one has an issue with the facility itself, but with the expensive way it was finished. Total waste of money," the older woman said, eyes twinkling innocently as she gathered small plates and serviettes. "A lot of us villagers questioned the cedar beams, the dressed stone finish, black, for heaven's sake, none of it was done on the cheap. Complete overkill and a waste of the taxpayer's money. The place looks like a high-end coffee shop or something like a ski resort in Whistler."

"Oh, I know what building you're talking about now. It's that new one out on the Whisky Corner Road. Customers were talking about it yesterday."

"Yeah, that's the one. Anyway, last night someone hung up a sign that read 'coming soon – Chicken and Rib Extravaganza', right over the entrance." Gladys chuckled.

"And you had nothing to do with it?" Maisy sounded doubtful.

"I only held the ladder." Her grandmother smiled mischievously and then sipped her coffee. Straightening, she waved a hand at the tea towel covered dough lined up in rectangular metal pans. "I have to let this batch rise for an hour, grab the butter and we'll have breakfast on the patio." Gladys took a tray down from the black hooks on the wall and added the items to carry outside.

The patio attached to Gladys' unit overlooked the marina and the waters of the Samsum Narrows. There was always something interesting to see. The boats, the people and what they were up to in the marina, or, when all was quiet, the view. Today, the plumbing van was again parked by the marina entrance, across from the condo building driveway.

Maisy picked up her coffee and the butter dish, adding then to the tray beside the dishes and napkins. Two steps into the living area, she came to an abrupt halt. "Holy crap, what the heck is that?"

Gladys peered over her granddaughter's shoulder. "Oh, my, it's a trapdoor spider. They're harmless, but don't move, you'll startle it and he'll run under the furniture." She put her tray down on the counter. "I do NOT want a five-inch spider under my couch."

Slowly, Gladys eased her way around the circumference of the room.

"How would something that big get in here? Did we leave the patio door open?"

Gladys frowned as she edged carefully around Maisy trying not to startle the arachnid. "I don't think I did. I'm usually very careful not to leave the place unlocked. Especially since the thefts started." Gladys rolled her bottom lip over her teeth as she moved toward the glass doors.

Abruptly, the spider ran to the right.

Both women shrieked and then look sheepishly at each other when the spider paused under the coffee table.

"You can hear it run across the floor, that's so freaky." Maisy stepped slowly away from the glass top wicker table. She kept her eyes glued on the spider. "That's the biggest, weirdest arachnid I've ever seen. If that thing moves toward me, I am out of here."

"Where's Albert?"

Maisy glanced quickly over her shoulder and back again. "He's sleeping in his basket."

Strange noises were emanating from the cat, even though he was four feet off the floor on his cat post. Blofeld had his face lowered, with only his eyes and ears poking up over the curved side of his sleeping platform.

"What's wrong with Blofeld?"

"I don't know, usually he will tackle any bug." Gladys leaned over the armchair to reach the patio door handle.

"Maybe this spider is too big for him?"

"He brings me snakes."

"Oh. Well, I guess spiders are scarier. What's the plan?" Maisy swallowed, still staring at the multiple eyes looking right back at her.

"Since the cat is too afraid to chase the spider, I'm hoping if I open the patio doors, it will make a run for freedom." She frowned at the lock. It was already open. All Gladys had to do was press down the door lever. She must have left it open last night after all, but she could distinctly remember checking the doors were locked before she left with Arlie. At least, she thought she had.

"Okay, good plan. I'm just glad it's not going to come this way."

"You hope." Gladys chuckled and moved her hand up to the handle. "You never know what a creature will do."

"You have a mean streak, you know that?"

"Yeah, that's what Arlie says too." She pressed the lever and inch by inch, eased the door open.

"It's moving!" The girl backed up and the spider stopped its scuttle toward her.

Maisy bumped an article of furniture and a feline squawk sounded above and behind her. "Sorry, Blofeld."

"He's got nothing to complain about." Gladys had one door open. "Dealing with spiders is Blofeld's job." She toed off her shoes and gingerly stepped up onto the seat of the armchair.

"What do we do now?"

"We wait."

"Seriously? I don't think so."

"Maisy–"

"Shoo!" Maisy waved her coffee mug and the butter dish at the spider as she leaned forward.

The wee beast scuttled the opposite direction, out the door, over the threshold, and out to freedom. The spider kept going with an odd clattering sound as it zipped across the concrete patio. The creature disappeared under the leaves of the ferns that were the backdrop for the flowerbeds.

Collectively, the women released a long breath.

Blofeld stood up to look around. He performed one turn on his post, and curled up again, eyes mere slits of green as if satisfied his job was done.

Gladys stepped off the wicker chair and turned a stern eye on the huge white Persian. "Blofeld." She stabbed a finger at the feline. "You're fired."

Maisy laughed.

Gladys picked up the tray and Maisy led the way outside. They settled down in the shade of an Arbutus tree. They laid out their breakfast on the round glass top table and took seats in the matching chairs.

Butter was liberally applied and promptly melted, dripping on to Gladys's plate as she nibbled her breakfast.

"Maisy, did you stay here all evening?"

"No, but I wasn't gone long. I took Linda's cloths up to her place." She used her knife to cut off more of the raspberry bread. "Of course, I helped her move some furniture too. I doubt I was gone more than an hour. Why?"

Gladys shook her head. "Just thinking." She glanced at her slim wristwatch. "It's almost seven-thirty."

"What happens at seven-thirty?"

"The morning fashion show begins." Gladys refilled their coffee cups and found her granddaughter giving her a reproving look. "Don't look at me like that. I take my entertainment as it comes. People watching is how I find out if I might gain a customer or two from the boater traffic. Ones that encourage nightly visitors are not usually in the market for fresh, home baked bread the next morning, but vacationing boaters and the sailing clubs usually welcome it."

"Would this be live-aboard boat people or the visitors dock people?" Maisy popped a morsel into her mouth and chewed.

"Sometimes a bit of both," Gladys commented.

"Aha." Maisy said, sounding uncertain.

"I'm not spying on the neighbours. I'm obtaining business leads."

"Sure," her granddaughter said.

"Withhold judgement until you've seen today's show." Gladys gestured to the north end of the boat finger docks. "Wait for it."

A woman in her late forties and on the largish side with long dark-hair appeared. She was tall as well as broad. She sauntered down the dock carrying a bag and towel in her right hand while her left, was pointed out and up, as though she held an invisible long stem cigarette holder. This was not the most remarkable thing, however.

"Oh. My." Maisy said.

"Yes." Gladys' lips quirked up, her granddaughter delivered the phrase similar to how she, herself would have it.

The woman was trailed by an equally tall and broad blond male. His long hair was caught up in a knot on the back of his head. They each wore a fuzzy fleece onesie complete with red and white horizontal stripes. 'Thing 1' was clearly printed in large white letter across her back, and her possible spouse sported 'Thing 2' on his.

"Heh, cute." Maisy said and tore off another chunk of raspberry bread.

Gladys chuckled. "I have to admit the onesies are a bit better than a bathrobe."

"Where are they headed?"

"I believe they're going to the showers." Each was carrying a small vinyl bag the right size for toiletries along with their towels.

Maisy picked up her coffee for a sip. "The fun just never stops around here," she said dryly, but stopped with her cup halfway to her mouth and she stared.

Gladys looked in the direction the girl's gaze was stuck.

Some distance away, on the live-aboard dock at the marina, a white-haired man well over eighty, walked briskly down his dock following the first woman and man. He merely wore a bright orange towel slung around his skinny hips, and neon orange flip-flops on his bare feet. He carried a green cloth grocery bag with a white towel half visible over the top of the bag.

"Every day I wonder if today's the day the orange towel slips." Gladys said to the sound of the man's flip-flops snapping against the wooden docks. The water was a great conductor of sound, along with the bowl shape of the land surrounding the marina.

"Eeep." Maisy said and brought the mug to her mouth for a sip. After she swallowed, she looked at her grandmother. "You do this every morning, sit here and people watch the marina?"

"Well, not every morning," Gladys allowed. "Most days I'm too busy, but I have been more regularly since the star of our show berthed his boat on the visitors' dock a couple days ago." She gestured with a wave of her cup in the direction of a sailboat boat currently occupying its slip at the fifty-foot transient dock. The sailboat was a thirty-two-foot Bayfield, cutter rigged. Albion's Wish was written in script on the stern.

"Ah." Gladys smiled warmly, eyes on a male figure emerging from the cockpit.

Maisy tipped her head Gladys' way and curiously watched too.

A strikingly tall, fit man with short black hair and a healthy tan straighten up as he gained the dock. The young man wore a faded and ragged, grey T-shirt which clung to his trim muscled frame and tan walking shorts, these too were torn, and stained. They did reveal glimpses of long muscular legs dusted with black hair. On his feet were black sports sandals. He too carried a towel and small black bag.

"Wow." Maisy breathed as she watched the male stroll down the dock in the same direction as the others. He moved like an athlete, sure of what he was capable of.

"Wait for it..." Gladys held up one finger watching Maisy.

He turned the corner to access the main dock and Maisy could finally see his face. Involuntarily, her eyes widened as she stared. Her lips parted. Then the man disappeared from view behind marina office. Maisy cut her eyes to the older woman. "That's Ian Travers."

"Yes," Gladys said lifting her eyebrows slightly, gauging Maisy's reaction.

"His hair is cut so short I didn't recognize him until he turned our way completely."

"He said he had it cut for his next role. Some superhero movie that starts shooting in Vancouver in a couple of weeks. I think he likes it this way too, it's harder for people to recognize him."

Maisy stared at Gladys. "You were talking to him?"

"Yes, he told me when I asked. He's one of my customers. I made some flax bread for him." A pleased expression lit her round face. "He's due for another delivery tomorrow." She gave Maisy an innocent look.

Chapter Ten

Gladys placed her gunmetal-grey change box in a neon-green fabric grocery bag. It rested next to her half-sized clipboard which contained customer order sheets, a tablecloth and other items she might need for the farmer's market the marina.

She looped the bag over her wrist and picked up the last rack of bread and buns. The market was held in the courtyard between the restaurant and the mini strip mall made up of various businesses which made a living from selling goods and services to boaters.

After breakfast, Maisy had taken Albert out for his morning walk. They had taken the marina road, of course but Maisy hadn't caught a second glimpse of Ian Travers she'd told her grandmother with evident disappointment.

The wee dog was returned to Matthew's condo for his nap. Before heading to work, Maisy extracted a promise from her grandmother to at some point, introduce her to Ian Travers.

Her grandmother had smiled and of course agreed. Probably, it was the prospect of meeting the celebrity, which got Maisy's mind off starting her new job. She didn't mention she was nervous again, which had been the whole point of Gladys' strategy.

For market day, Gladys was dressed in tan capris-pants and a sage green tank top with a matching cardigan. Sometimes it could become coolish by the water. She wore her roman-style russet-coloured leather sandals with the flat soles. You never knew how long you'd be on your feet at the market, it was important to be comfortable.

She'd love a quick sellout, this had happened a time or two, but nothing was guaranteed. At a minimum, she would be at the marina market for a couple of hours.

Gladys hesitated by the hallway door and then decisively put her burdens back down on the table and briskly crossed the apartment to check if she'd locked the patio doors.

She was pleased to find she had. "I'm just being careful, not paranoid," she muttered this to herself as she picked up her things and took the last load of baking out to the car.

While the trap-door spider had been icky, far worse was the feeling she'd absentmindedly left the patio doors unlock. That was the downside of getting older, but Gladys was certain she had not forgotten. However, then it occurred to her that if that were true, maybe her apartment could have been broken into by the thief currently troubling the village. The idea struck her as so logical, Gladys waited until her granddaughter went to work to do a quick walk through of her apartment. She had not found anything missing.

The exercise told her nothing. Maybe her fifteen-year-old television was not worth the trouble, nor maybe the laptop she'd gotten second hand from her son back in 2013.

The uncertainty of whether somebody had come into her home while she was out was disturbing to say the least.

Someone must have opened the patio door and left it open for the spider to get in, she was sure of it. How else could the arachnid gotten into the condo? The patio screen door was never left open. At least she didn't think so.

Gladys had said none of this to Maisy. The girl had enough on her mind starting her first real job and it was all conjecture by her grandmother anyway. Still, Gladys couldn't shake the certainty someone must have broken in. She didn't own much of any great value, but if her dough mixer went missing, she would be hooped. The heavy, industrial size machine was top of the line, and cost over three hundred dollars. Replacing it, even with insurance money, would take time and negatively impact her business. Then of course, her insurance rates would go up too.

Baking rack balanced on one hip, she plucked her keys off the black stainless-steel hook attached to a wooden key rack. Micky had constructed the rack years ago in their garage. He'd decided to turn his hand to blacksmithing, with superb results. She rubbed her fingers over the black leaf key fob. The leaf, along with the hooks, were also from Micky's forge. The familiarity of the harden steel in her hand was reassuring. She exited the condo and locked that door too.

"Hello, there." Linda walked across to her from stairwell. She was dressed in navy walking shorts and a white knit top. Her black purse was hanging from her shoulder. Linda's blonde hair was pulled back into a ponytail, and she wore pale melon lipstick.

"How's it going?" Gladys smiled at her neighbour.

"Better, I'm going to see my insurance guy. Frank got all my repairs done and I want to see if I can get reimbursed. She gestured to a manila tab file folder poking out the top of her purse. "Frank gave me an invoice." Linda opened the back door for them. "I told him you were interested in getting your place inspected. He said to tell you he'll call you Monday to set up a time."

"Thank you, I appreciate that, but it's not necessary." Gladys carried her burden past her neighbour, and they turned down the walk which led to their cars parked in their assigned spaces in the lot.

They reached the station wagon. "It was not trouble, thanks for helping me with my latest disaster." Linda gave her a little wave and continued on to her white mid-sized two-door sedan on the other side of visitors' parking.

Gladys had left the rear gate of the car unlocked so she merely had to heave it open to slide the last rack in next to the first ones.

The sound of the basement metal garage door ratcheting opening drew her attention as she closed the back of her station wagon.

Lara Finkle, long blonde hair flowing in the wind from the speed of her exit, emerged from the underground garage driving her red convertible. She was wearing a bright-pink sheath dress which matched her flashy fuchsia manicure. The car continued past Gladys and Linda without so much as a look, let alone a wave from Lara.

The sports car was ten feet from the end of the driveway when the brake lights flashed red to slow the vehicle. A brown Plymouth accelerated up the Coast Road at the same time.

Abruptly, the driver of the brown car turned onto the approach and headed down the drive. The vehicle came to a stop mere inches in front of Lara's bumper and effectively blocked the exit.

Gladys frowned as she watched the bald male. He was the same guy she'd seen only yesterday, Vinny Norquay. He confronted her second-floor neighbour with a shout. "You need to talk to me."

Lara flipped him the bird and honked her horn at him in anger. "Move your stupid car."

Vinny opened his driver-side door.

Gladys exchanged a look with Linda, she too, would be delayed.

Lara looked startled when Vinny got out of his vehicle. The situation also looked like it might get ugly fast.

The man's lined face looked haggard. His faded beige T-shirt was sweat stained under the arms and there was a damp patch on his chest. His jeans and boots might have seen better days, but that would have been long in the past.

Two quick strides brought him over to the driver side of her vehicle. "You haven't returned my calls or answer any of my messages." Vinny's words were heated.

Gladys didn't like the ugly expression on the fifty-something man's face either.

"You're avoiding me." His words traveled quite clearly to Gladys.

She needed to get to the marina for the market. Although she was curious about the scene playing out in front of her, she couldn't leave with the brown car blocking the driveway anyway.

Now Vinny braced his hands on Lara's door and leaned down to scowled at her. "Where's my money?" he said, pushing the words out from between clenched teeth.

Lara leaned away and hastily wound up the window. Like that would do any good. The woman had nowhere to go and no protection with the convertible top down.

Apprehension crept up Gladys' spine and she was tempted to go over there. Lara wasn't the nicest person at the best of times, but was she in trouble? It might be good if Gladys let Vinny know she was here, at least as a witness, in case the angry man had something nefarious planned.

Then Lara lifted her chin. "You'll get your money." She appeared to have recovered her confidence. "This is not the time, nor the place to speak about this, Vinny."

Gladys realized the other woman was not frightened; she was angry. Still, Gladys kept an eye on the pair of them as she walked up to the driver's door of the station wagon and opened it. Maybe she should drive up behind Lara? Should she take photos? It's what everyone else seemed to do in strange and unusual situations like this.

Gladys fished her phone out of the green cloth bag and put the bag down on the driver's seat so she could use both hands.

"I did the job. I want my money." Vinny was saying.

"You'll get your payment. Now move that rusting heap, I have somewhere to be."

Both were unaware Gladys took several photographs of the cars, their license plates, and the drivers. Just in case things go out of control. You never knew.

Vinny leaned in closer, over top of the closed window. "It's been six months. Dwayne said you were good for it. You own me, plus interest."

Lara waved her hand at him. "Yes, yes, all right. I have to liquidate a few things to get you your money. That's where I'm off to, the bank. You'll have to wait a day or two for my investments to be cashed out and the transfer to be executed."

Gladys tucked her phone away again. It sounded to her like the two were well acquainted.

"That's not good enough. I've been very patient with you. Give me my bloody money!"

"I said I'd pay you. I just told you I'm going to my bank."

He narrowed his eyes at Lara as she studied her. "How's about I go to the bank with you?" It wasn't a question. It also didn't sound like Lara was going to be given much of a choice. The good news was Vinny did sound calmer, almost mollified, even if his words did sound snide.

"Fine, all right." Lara flicked her right index finger at the Plymouth blocking the driveway. "Move your car, then." Her left hand dropped down to the gear shift. "Park back there in visitor parking." Her pink lacquered right thumb jerked over her shoulder to indicate an open parking space.

Vinny stared down at her for a moment more, like he didn't trust her. "Okay, then." He shoved himself away from her vehicle and returned to his car.

"Hurry up." Lara's words were laced with annoyance. "The ferry will be leaving any minute now. We want to make the boat and get this done today."

He waved a dismissive acknowledgement and got behind the wheel of the running sedan. Slowly, Vinny eased his car past Lara's on the narrow gravel driveway, and then headed to an empty visitor space. The Plymouth's back bumper had just barely cleared Lara's when she gunned the engine and floored the accelerator to charge up the drive.

Lara didn't stop to check for on-coming traffic. There was a screeching of tires as she made contact with the Coast Road's paved surface. The red convertible shot past the plumbing van parked on the road by the marina entrance. The vehicle roared up the street to the first bend and was gone.

Vinny swore loudly and then hastily backed out of the parking lot. He performed a quick, tight U-turn and give chase. Unfortunately, once the hood of the car was aimed for the exit, he hit the accelerator probably a little too hard. The rear wheels spun on the graveled driveway, causing the back end of his car to dogleg. The front bumper clipped one of the spruce trees at the edge of the road. The impact brought the vehicle to a sudden halt.

Gladys glanced at her watch as Vinny backed up again and finally made it to the road. The mid-morning ferry might still be loading when Vinny got there, but she doubted it.

Lara was unreasonably lucky when it came to her own self-interest. Things just seemed to go her way. Which most times, seemed unfair to Gladys. Lara was not a decent person by anyone's definition. Still, Gladys hoped nothing bad happened to her.

She wondered what Vinny had done for Lara that she owed him money. Merely going by his road-rage, it must be a significant amount of money.

What did he mean by 'the job'? It sounded as though Dwayne Davis was somehow involved in their dispute, too. All very odd to say the least.

Vinny had been furious from the start. By the time he caught up with Lara he might be explosive. At least the ferry was a public place. Otherwise, it looked like karma might actually catch up with Lara after all this time, but who knew? The woman was a slippery character.

"What do you think that was about?" Linda called over to Gladys. She nodded to the Plymouth only now disappearing around the bend.

Gladys shook her head. "I have no idea." She moved the bag from the driver's seat to the passenger's. "Whatever it is, it can't be anything good." She slid behind the wheel.

"I hope Lara isn't going to get him to do any work for her."

Gladys raised her eyebrows in surprise at Linda's remark. "Why do you say that?"

"He's not a very good plumber. I think that's the guy who hooked up my washing machine."

Chapter Eleven

It only took Gladys and her station wagon all of two minutes to drive the short distance to the location of the farmer's market at the marina. The Coast Road was empty of traffic, so it was merely a matter of crossing the road and continuing downhill to the parking lot.

Even though it may have been quicker to walk to her destination, carrying all the items for the market, plus the restaurant order would have been a bit much for anyone. Gladys had no wish to put her back out carting bread racks around.

She parked the car in the public lot by the paved open area. The courtyard was formed by the marina office and the restaurant on the east side, the boat brokerage, and a marine specialty store on the west side. The parking lot opened into the courtyard from the south and a green space rested on the north side. Gladys noted over a dozen wooden planters were placed in various locations along the parameter. These were new. Although red geraniums were the dominate flower, each planter was bursting with a cornucopia of colour and scents. A nice improvement.

She stretched her neck to see the area she usually set up her space. Clustered in the middle of the courtyard space were picnic tables. Six were positioned in a ragged line. People were just beginning to mill about.

Satisfied, Gladys cut the engine just as Dwayne Davis coasted down the hill in his gold Chrysler. He smoothly docked the car two rows in front of her. She doubted Dwayne was at the marina for the market. He loudly disapproved of her cottage business at each condo meetings and had never purchased so much as a dinner roll from her.

He was out of luck if he thought he could stop her from running her bakery business. This was precisely the reason she sat on the condo board. Besides, the province and municipality allowed cottage business of all kinds.

As she got out of the car, she noted other vendors were setting up for the market too. Hastily she counted the picnic tables. Five were now taken. Farmers' market was a bit of a misnomer, it was more of an artisans' fair.

A middle-aged purple-haired woman, in matching purple cotton blouse and a long lilac skirt was arranging her five by seven water colours of the mountains, ocean, and sunsets. At the table next door, in front of the marine supply store, there was a slightly older silver-haired woman arranging jams and jellies in colourful glass jars. Gladys smiled at the woman's T-shirt slogan, 'Sticky & Sweet', it matched the labels on the front of the jars and the sign hanging from the front of her table.

A younger man worked directly across from the jam lady. He was unpacking wooden carvings of faces, small wooden toys, like cars, trucks, and sailboats. Another woman next to him had an enormous display of candles and crystals. Someone else offered handmade jewelry from beach stones but was not currently manning their table. The courtyard was quickly filling up with locals, boaters, and a few visitors. There was a cart selling mini sugar doughnuts and another, offering local wines.

Some of the coffee cup carrying crowd milled around a few of the displays but most sat in the spring sun enjoying the day. There was still fifteen minutes until the start of the market at ten.

Gladys needed to grab that last table. The marina only allowed six to be used for the market day. She grabbed her tablecloth and the sign to stake her claim to the last open space before making the restaurant delivery. She threaded her way through the bustle of the market. The good weather had brought lots of customers.

She took the white-painted picnic table close to the restaurant and leaned her sandwich board sign against one side.

"Gladys, it's about time you got here. We've been waiting for you."

She turned to see who addressed her. It was Earl Moffatt and another man who looked familiar, but she could not make his name come to her. "Hello there," she waved a general greeting. "It's not even ten o'clock, Earl. Anyway, what else have you got to do?" She knew the man liked to come off gruff but enjoyed a bit of teasing too. So, she gave as good as she got.

The pair of grizzled seventy-plus males ambled over to her. "Ed and I have things to do all right, don't you worry. Come on, come on, setup your stall. Did you bring cinnamon rolls?"

"I did, but I have to make a delivery to Holly before I set up."

"Get after it, woman. I'm only here for your baking." Earl said this with a stern expression. Anyone who was familiar with former undertaker knew this was what passed as humour for him.

"Hold your horses. I'll be back in a minute. Make yourself useful and spread out my tablecloth, and open my sign please."

"Work, work, work." Earl remarked to his friend as Gladys returned to her car.

The contents of the first rack were for the restaurant kitchen. She took up the fresh baked breads and walked over to the back entrance. The screen door was the only barrier. The back security door was open to allow air flow. The tempting aroma of bacon cooking greeted her, and then so too did Holly, the restaurant manager of the Blue Heron.

"Hi Gladys, use this prep table to unload." She gestured to the stainless-steam flat surface.

"Thanks, Holly." She began unloading the bags of buns and loaves while Holly sorted. Most went into upright freezer, a few she left on the prep table.

"Thanks, see you Friday." Holly handed Gladys the payment envelope.

"And thank you for your business." Gladys grinned at the restaurant manager and tucked the cheque into her right front pocket.

Two minutes later, Gladys was back at the rear of her car. She opened the gate and saw the back was empty. No bread or rolls were left in the back. Empty racks were stacked, one on the other, and the scent of fresh bread was the only evidence her products were ever in the car.

For a fraction of a second, a horrible feeling washed over her, the same as when she realized somebody had been in her home uninvited. Then she had the presence of mind to look over at her table.

"Gladys," Earl called when he spotted her.

The umbrella was open, her tablecloth spread out and the bakery items were placed on the table directly under the sun protection. Earl was waving a twenty-dollar bill at her over the heads of several customers queuing up.

She grabbed the green bag with her change box and hurried over. The sign, a professional job, was opened and placed at a good visible angle. It sported graphics of bread loaves cooling surrounding her business name, Gladys' Baked Goods. One corner displayed the prices and the types of products offered. Quickly the sign and the table were obscured by her many customers.

Earl and Ed were doing a brisk business. "Can you break a twenty?"

"Of course," Gladys laughed and opened the cash box to do just that.

Inside of twenty minutes all the baking was sold, and Gladys' cash box was nicely filled.

"Thanks for your help, boys."

Earl's friend Ed grinned. "No problem, thanks for the discount." He made his way over to the jam lady who was doing well too.

Earl lingered to chat as Gladys folded the tablecloth. "Helping let us put dibs on your cinnamon buns." She chuckled as she slid the folded material into her bag.

"You know, Gladys, you should think of opening your own bakery." Earl suggested as he picked up her sign and walked with it to her car.

"I've thought about it, but–"

The heavy oak door which led to the pub side of the restaurant swung open and crashed against the wall.

Both Gladys and Earl paused, as did several other people in the courtyard, to check out the commotion in the doorway of the bar.

"Get out. I told you before about peddling your crap in my bar." A large blond man wrapped in a white cotton apron prodded Dwayne Davis over the threshold. His fair complexion was flushed, right up and over his buzz cut.

"Chris is upset," Gladys commented.

While the barman was flushed in the face, he was not nearly as red in the face as Dwayne.

"Stop coming in here and bothering my customers. No one wants your junk." The bartender wore a light-blue dress shirt with the sleeves rolled up over his biceps, displaying muscle and dark tattoos. "You try that again and I'll ban you from the premises."

Dwayne walked backward clutching his cardboard box and nodded. "Sorry, Chris."

Gladys realized her neighbour wasn't just angry, he was embarrassed too.

His posture appeared contrite as his big hands flexed against the contours of the box. "It won't happen again."

Big Chris grunted and turned his back on the older man, and then disappeared into the dim interior of the bar.

Ponderously, the wooden door with a brass port hole, swung shut behind him.

Dwayne looked over at the collection of people watching the scene. He straightened his back and gave the people watching him an ugly look. Her neighbour then turned on his boot heel and strode away to the parking lot.

"The entertainment appears to be over," Earl said.

"Looks that way." Gladys continued on to her car.

Across the wide expanse of pavement, the Cordoba swung out of the lot. Dwayne had the top down and he maneuvered the vehicle past them and took the hill at significant speed, barely pausing at the stop sign before pulling onto the road.

"He's still driving that gas guzzler like he stole it. Which doesn't make sense with his money problems."

Gladys fished her keys out of her left pocket. "How do you know Dwayne is having financial troubles?"

"He makes the rounds every week. Looking for someone to buy the second-hand stuff he has for sale. I usually see him at the seniors' centre, but he stops by the bar here all the time too. My grandson buses tables and works in the kitchen. Sean said once the cops were called because of a dispute over ownership. A radar and chart plotter system Dwayne was selling was allegedly stolen off of someone's boat. The prospective customer was the victim of said theft, or so Sean said."

She raised her eyebrows in shock. "Was Dwayne charged?"

"No, the serial numbers didn't match."

"Not the stolen items, then."

"So, the story goes. Anyway, after that, Chris tried to put a lid on Dwayne selling stuff in the bar."

"When was this?"

"This past February."

"Couldn't Dwayne be selling things from his own boat?"

Earl lifted one grey eyebrow at Gladys. "His boat was repossessed back in January." He nodded at her car. "How's the old Forrester running?"

Chapter Twelve

After a quick trip to the bank to deposit the day's earnings, Gladys made a stop at the post office. She collected her mail, and then pushed open the heavy wood and glass door which led to the inner part of the building. The postal assistants usually worked behind the old-fashioned wickets. Today, no one was about at either window.

Gladys was about to call out to let the staff know she was there when she heard conversation.

"Ha, I see wood." That was Donna, the new postmaster.

There was a long pause. "What?" Carin answered carefully.

"I meant, I can see my desk, get your mind out of the gutter."

Carin laughed wickedly and so did Gladys.

She figured it was time to let them know they were not alone. "Hello!"

Donna popped out of the office, slightly red-cheeked. "Hi Gladys, how can I help?"

Gladys smiled innocently back. "A package of business size stamped envelopes, please."

The postmaster was quick to fulfill the request. "Have you heard the latest?"

"Probably not." Gladys put a twenty on the counter. She hadn't seen Arlie today. He kept her up to speed on local happenings. Well, the gossip anyway.

"Oh, well it's to do with one of your condo neighbours." Donna opened the cash register to make change. "Lara Finkle was robbed."

"Yeah, I had heard that a day or so ago." Gladys slid the envelops into her green cloth bag. She liked to mail in her quarterly tax payments and second quarter was coming up.

"Word at the seniors centre is that she lost a huge chunk of money and some jewelry. Not that there is much sympathy for her."

Gladys took her change and receipt and tucked both in a pocket. "No, I wouldn't think there would be. Lara doesn't go out of her way to get along with people. Still, these robberies are a terrible thing."

"A couple have happened right in your building. Do they make you feel unsafe?"

Gladys pursed her lips as she thought about it. "No, but it is unsettling." She collected her envelops. "There's been stuff stolen from all over the village, not just on Coast Road."

"That's true," Donna agreed.

Carin exited the mail sorting area and joined them. "My neighbour Shelley, one of her hand sculptures was stolen right out of her yard."

"The giant white ones?" Donna turned to her co-worker.

"The same. Jenn, next door to Shelley, her rotor tiller is missing." Carin said. "I also heard Keith Blacksmith thought someone tried to steal the tailgate from his old blue truck."

Gladys frowned. "Is something like that valuable?"

"Apparently so," Carin shrugged. "The truck's a '77. The thief couldn't get the tailgate off because Keith said he'd spot welded the bolts or screws or something."

"Good idea. Anything not nailed down seems to be a target." Donna said and blandly looked back at Gladys. "I wonder if the banners on the new pump house have anything to do with the robberies."

"I doubt it." Gladys said quickly. "The banners are harmless pranks. Stealing from people points to a lower-class life form. See you later." She got out of there pronto.

After the post office, Gladys returned home and parked the station wagon back in its spot.

She was pleased to have the rest of the day to do as she liked. Maybe she'd take Albert out for a walk, just like the young couple she'd passed on the road home. It was a lovely day for it. Gladys grabbed her stuff out of the car and locked up.

Lately, it felt like all she did was bake things and sell them. Retirement was not exactly shaping up to be what she had expected. In her mind she was working harder now than when she had been a ward clerk at the hospital.

Gladys trudged through the condo building's back door. Her social life had dwindled to almost nothing. Running a small business wasn't the best way to live, but what else could she do? Her pension from work didn't cover all her expenses. Anyway, it was best to stay busy, wasn't it?

A walk in the sunshine would be good exercise and a lovely break. Then afterward, figure out something for supper. A barbeque on the patio might be nice, or a lovely spaghetti dinner with garlic bread and salad. Pasta was Maisy's favourite. It would be good to take the rest of the day off for once.

The building manager's door swung open as Gladys walked over to her own door. Enid Lindquist exited her apartment and closed the door sharply behind her. She carried several sheets of paper in her left hand.

A feeling of impending doom dropped on Gladys as she watched Enid stride across the hallway. "Gladys, excellent, I was hoping you would be back soon." The building manager must have been watching for her to time their meeting so perfectly.

"Hello, Enid." Gladys set down the racks on the floor and dug for her keys in her green bag. Apparently, Enid held no ill will toward Gladys after their heated words from the day before.

The other woman thrust one of the sheets of paper in front of Gladys' face. "Here is the agenda for tonight's condo meeting."

Cautiously, Gladys straightened and took the proffered printed agenda. She gave Enid a weak smile. "Thanks."

"I decided to move up the monthly meeting because of the events of yesterday."

"Right." Gladys grimaced a smile at the building manager. With more resignation than curiosity she glanced at the bullet points.

· Building Water damage
· Building security
· Running a business from a residence
· Pets

The last two bullet points made Gladys frown. "What's this about businesses and pets?" The agenda items also guaranteed she'd be present at the meeting to make sure Dwayne and Enid didn't ram some new bylaw in that precluded her running her bakery or having a pet. She couldn't even think about giving up Blofeld.

Then there was the matter of Albert. She needed to contact Matthew. He needed to know what was going on.

"Now Gladys," Enid said with a patronizing tone. "Not everyone likes yappy–"

The front doors swung open, and a pair of strangers strolled into the foyer. Enid's next words were stalled as she zeroed in the on the non-residents.

They were the young couple Gladys had seen walking along Coast Road earlier. The man and the woman were in their twenties, and both carried heavy-duty taupe backpacks. The packs were stuffed to the seams as though all their worldly goods were jammed inside. Each wore a white T-shirt, ragged jean shorts, and sport sandals with heavy tread, good for hiking.

They looked at the condo residents. "Hello." They both said at the same time to Enid and Gladys. Then the dark-haired male advanced to the elevator with his ginger-haired girlfriend on his heels.

He reached for the elevator call button.

Enid sprinted forward and swatted his hand away.

"Hey," his girlfriend objected.

"The elevator is out of commission until it can be inspected." The building manager dug in her left skirt pocket and removed a ring of keys. She inserted one into the button panel of the elevator and locked it out. "Can't you read the sign?" she snapped at the pair.

Gladys opened her mouth to remind Enid that Norm had shut off the elevator's breakers, but then noticed the floor number display panel above the elevator was lit. Someone must have reset the breakers. Probably Enid, the control freak.

The young strangers both leaned forward to look at the small paper sign taped above the call buttons. Gladys was surprised Enid hadn't locked out the elevator before this if it was so dangerous.

"Oh, okay then," the male said. "We can take the stairs." His girlfriend shrugged in amiable agreement.

Enid held up one hand to stop them. "You are not residents. Who are you?" Her tone was downright rude as she leveled a narrowed-eyed look on the pair.

Gladys stepped forward to deflect the manager's hostile attitude. "Obviously, these young people are visitors, Enid. Don't be so unfriendly." Gladys offered a smile to the newcomers. "Are you here visiting Freddie or maybe to see Linda?" She raised her eyebrows in inquiry.

The pair shook their heads.

"Surely not Lara Finkle?" Enid sounded confident.

The young woman blinked at her. "We don't know anyone here. We hitchhiked from Ganges. We're just staying in a place upstairs."

"What do you mean, staying in someone's unit?" Enid took an aggressive step forward.

The young man blinked at her. "We booked the Airbnb. We're staying in 203 for one night." He flashed an uncertain grin at them. "Tomorrow, we're taking the ferry to Stoney Mountain. Come on, Lovey, let's go get settled. I'm dying for a shower." He led the way to the stairwell exit. The condo owners watched nonplused as the young couple ascended the stairs.

"An Airbnb in 203." Gladys said uncertainly. "They're talking about the unsold unit."

Freddie exited past the two hitchhikers and extended a friendly hello, which they returned.

Gladys turned to Enid as the young couple disappeared around the corner. "Someone bought 203?" she asked.

Freddie paused next to Gladys. He looked between the two women. No doubt having heard her question.

Enid compressed her thin lips into an even thinner line. "As far as I know, condo unit 203 still belongs to the condominium corporation. I've not heard any different."

Curiosity sparkled in Freddie's eyes. "What's the problem?" He slid his hands in the front pockets of his jeans. "Or is this juicy gossip?"

Gladys turned to him. "Someone is renting out a unit in the building."

"So? We are allowed to sublet if we want. Matthew has your granddaughter staying in his place while he's away."

"That's not the same thing." Gladys gave Freddie a dry look. "Maisy's not renting, she's housesitting."

Enid jabbed a finger upward. "Airbnbs are NOT allowed in this building. I can't believe Pink Brick would have set up any unit for short term rental. There has to be a mistake or something."

"Apparently they did." Freddie shrugged his thin shoulders. "Some furniture was delivered two weeks ago. I saw people from 'Your New Home'. They set up the unit," Freddie said. "I thought maybe they were staging the place for an open house, but no one ever came out to look as far as I know."

"When was this? I never saw those people," Enid said sharply.

"They were here the same time as the drywall contractors when they were putting together the estimate for Dwayne's place after Linda's hot water heater blew. There was lots of comings and goings, you might not have noticed."

Enid's fingers curled into fists. Her right hand crumpled the meeting agendas she held. "Renting out any unit like a hotel room is against the bylaws."

Gladys wondered whether the building manager's wrath was because the Airbnb was a breach of the building bylaws, or, and more likely, because the Enid was out of the loop when it came to up-to-date information with regard to the vacant apartment.

Enid jutted out her bottom jaw. "I'm going to contact Pink Brick this minute. This situation is unacceptable." She turned and grabbed the paper out of Gladys' hand. "This agenda needs to be updated too." She stalked away to her own unit and slammed the door.

Quiet filled the hallway. "I think another item has just been added to the agenda." Freddie waggled sun-lightened eyebrows at Gladys.

She signed and nodded in agreement. "I'm guessing it will be another contentious meeting."

GLADYS LET ALBERT INTO her condo and made sure the water and food dishes on the floor were full for him. Then move on to Blofeld's, which she now placed on the lid of her mini freezer, and well away from Albert's questing tongue. She had to do something. The dog was getting rounder by the day eating his food and the cat's food too.

Her walk had been lovely along the Coast Road under the spring sun and down onto the small beach where she'd let the terrier run to his heart's content. No one else was around, so where was the harm? It was also heartening to see the wee dog back to his pre-accident self. That is, if his injuries were the result of an accident.

She frowned in thought watching Albert gulp down water. He lifted his dripping muzzle to look up at her snorting and sniffing while he stood in the utility room doorway.

"Are you trying to be a submarine?"

Albert just looked back at her quizzically as water from his muzzle dripped on the floor.

Gladys shook her head with a short laugh. "Never mind, puppy." She grabbed the old towel put there for when Albert's feet were muddy and wiped up the water.

The dog snorted one more time, then trotted over to his basket and climbed in. Seconds later, he was snoring.

Heading back into the kitchen, she hung the leash from a hook on the key rack. Maisy would need it later for Albert's evening walk. She then sat down at her small desk and opened her laptop to see if she had a reply from Matthew. Thankfully, there was a new unread email from her younger neighbour. Gladys read it with a smile and printed off his reply to take with her to the meeting.

It was almost four o'clock, much later than Gladys had thought. Maisy would be home soon.

They would eat, do the dishes, and then at seven, Gladys would attend the dreaded condo board meeting in Enid's condo. It would be hot and stuffy unless she could convince the manager to open a couple of windows. Enid said she was allergic to pollen. She also didn't like the outdoors, so rarely used her patio, and never for company. She also didn't have any air conditioning, which was a pity. June was warming up quickly.

She heard a noise outside her door. A sheet of paper was slipped under the hallway door. This had to be the updated agenda. Gladys got up and walked over. She scooped up the paper to have a look and couldn't help but to roll her eyes as she read the three new items:

· Special assessment #3
· Airbnb prohibition
· Cannabis

There was no help for it, but at least she had Matthew's email. Since she was to attend the evening meeting, Gladys figured she'd better get a move on with preparing dinner and then get a quick shower.

THAT EVENING, GLADYS pulled on a clean blue cotton T-shirt that sported a dolphin on the front and stated the shirt's origin was Bloody Bay, Little Cayman Island. An old souvenir from her and Micky's scuba diving vacations. Micky had bought it for her. It was one hundred per cent cotton and very comfortable. Plus, the shirt was minus tomato sauce stains from the spaghetti dinner she'd prepared.

In the reflections of the mirror, she could see Albert was stretched out at the foot of the bed on the white and grey carpet. He'd taken to keeping her in his sight when Maisy was not around and hadn't been happy to be locked out of the bathroom earlier. Now he was watching her get ready.

He'd been walked again, so his energy level was down. Slowly, he rolled over on his side and let out a contented sigh.

Blofeld chose that moment to saunter into the bedroom. He stopped to stare hard at the dog.

Gladys paused in brushing her hair to watch the animal's interaction.

The dog studiously ignored his nemeses.

"Good boy, Albert."

Blofeld watched the dog like he was planning something.

"Be good, Blofeld." She addressed this to her cat.

The Persian sniffed disdainfully and then leapt up onto the bed to curl up into his regulation football shape in the middle of the duvet.

She was pleased the conflict between the two animals had dwindled. Maybe they were learning to co-exist. She went back to working the brush through her thick curls. Not so much chestnut anymore as light silver-grey. Still, she thought she'd gotten away lucky, her greying locks were a better alternative than her sister's situation. Betty had to dye her hair otherwise she'd have a white strip down the middle, just like a skunk, poor thing.

The temperature had climbed to 27 Celsius even though evening was closing in and it was a complete waste of heat in Gladys' opinion.

Earlier, even the bedroom windows had been opened. This measure was to keep her energy costs down, Gladys didn't want to run the air conditioner unless it was absolutely necessary.

All the windows were closed and locked now, except the bathroom windows, which were too small for anyone to get through. She would draw the blinds and put on a couple of fans to keep the animals comfortable before leaving the condo. There would be no risk of anyone gaining entry to her place, that was certain, nor Matthew Wilkes' apartment. She'd made sure her granddaughter had checked the windows and doors before she left to go out.

Maisy, at Gladys' urging, had accepted an invitation to watch some old movie in the park. This week at the café, Maisy had become acquainted with village councillor Celine Nickels' brother, Liam. He'd told her the community centre ran the movie event a couple times a week in summer. It would do the girl good to make some new friends. Since there wasn't much night life in Musgrave Landing, the movie in the park was as good as it got.

While it was true lots of young people made the trip to Ganges on the other side of Salt Spring Island for excitement, Maisy didn't know a lot of people yet. She also wasn't as outgoing as some her age either. Her granddaughter also didn't own a car and did not want to be seen behind the wheel of the Forester station wagon. Maisy's fussiness with her image made Gladys chuckle. When she was a girl, it didn't matter what anyone drove, as long as you had wheels and could get out of the village and away from parental eyes.

She'd spent a lot of her summers after work in her father's lumber yard, on the beach close to Smuggler's Cove. Most of the time she'd kept out of trouble or at least, she allowed, she hadn't been caught.

Over the years, as a mature member of the community, Gladys had attended the movies in the park a time or two with a friend. A good portion of the village usually turned up, with a mix of young and old. It was quite nice sitting on a blanket and watching an old Hitchcock movie. Later in the week the movie would be geared more for kids.

Blue eyes looked back at her as she finished brushing her hair. She just now realized her eyes and the T-shirt were exactly the same shade of blue. She blinked in surprise. Was this why Micky had picked this top for her? The thought made her smile fondly.

Chapter Thirteen

Twenty minutes later Gladys was seated on Enid Lindquist's uncomfortable lilac-purple love seat. She sat at one end, at a right angle from Linda, who had taken a place in one of the white and lilac armchairs. These matched a second armchair and a chesterfield, all the same pastel purple and undoubtable new going by the stiffness of the cushions. The furniture was arranged in a conversation circle around a low coffee table painted a dark purple hue.

She and Linda were waiting on Freddie and Dwayne. Lara never attended the meetings and was not expected. Gladys idly wondered if Lara was back from the bank and if Vinny had caught up with her at some point.

Enid was busy in her kitchen, putting together tea for the meeting. This was her usual ritual. Enid liked to use her antique sterling-silver tea service for company and Gladys had to admit the full display was quite something. It also put the building manager in such a pleasant mood no one had the guts to decline the beverage, the crust-less sandwiches, or petite fours which would follow.

The rigmarole would have been more appropriate around four-thirty in the afternoon, but it was Enid's show.

There were a couple quick raps on the door, and it opened. "Hi Enid, it's me!" Freddie called.

"Come in, Freddie, and have a seat." Enid called back.

He strode in with a smile for both Linda and Gladys. "Hello ladies." Freddie beamed at them and sat at the opposite end of the love seat from Gladys.

"Hello." Gladys returned his smile and extracted a set of black-framed glasses to perch on her nose. She then opened the leather folder she used to take notes and keep track of bylaws, amendments, and motions. She balanced it on her knees and wrote in the current date at the top of the page and added the list of attendees thus far.

Officially, she was the secretary for these meetings, and she didn't mind. It was easier to keep the board on track and honest if she had a record of the minutes.

At the last meeting three weeks ago, even before she'd moved in, Gladys had to call out Enid and Dwayne for hiring one of Enid's nephews to run the job of replacing all the hot water heaters that were the same brand and lot number as Linda's after her appliance had ruptured. This was the second and most damaging flood.

Matthew had found out the builder originally purchased the water heaters from a liquidation warehouse. Once this was known, the corporation insurance company feared that if one was faulty, chances were good the others water heaters were probably faulty too, so all were replaced.

"If you'd gotten three bids, and your nephew was experienced and reasonably priced, it wouldn't be a problem," Gladys had explained at that earlier meeting. "But he's none of those things and it's a conflict of interest. I move we go with

West Tech Plumbing." Matthew, Linda, and Freddie had voted with her, carrying the motion. That was how they'd met Frank Warren, the plumber.

"Hi, Freddie." Linda nodded at him.

With the windows shut and no cross ventilation it didn't take long for the pungent aroma of green weed to make Gladys' nose itch. At least she'd remembered to take something before the meeting. The medication would keep her allergies under control, at least to a certain extent. She'd tucked tissues in her pockets just in case too.

"I'm guessing you've both seen the plumbing company working across the road at the marina?" Freddie tipped his head in the general direction of the marina. "Do either of you know what they're working on?"

"No, they just showed up there sometime on Monday." Linda said. "I noticed them when I got home from town."

"We should take down their details. We might need another plumbing quote." Freddie said. He winked at Linda and plucked his T-shirt away from his chest. It was getting warm in Enid's apartment.

She gave Freddie a sour look. "Very funny. I like Frank, he does good work." Linda wanted nothing to do with any new plumbers. "If I ever need a plumber again, Frank will be who I'll call." She looked at Gladys. "Frank said you declined his services."

"I did. Arlie and Jack hooked up my appliances when I moved in. I'm confident my connections are fine but thank you for thinking of me." Gladys said with a smile to soften her words.

"Oh, well, you should have said you didn't need Frank." Linda frowned at Gladys like her feelings were hurt.

"She probably did, but you–" Freddie cut off his words as Enid pushed a wheeled cart fully decked out with the tea service.

Gladys patted Freddie's arm to let him know the matter was closed.

The sterling-silver tea service gleamed, and the gold-edged china rattled faintly as Enid pushed the cart over the edge of the area carpet. The trolley held the full shebang, complete with tiny tongs for the sugar lumps. There was a three-tiered cake plate and tiny confections were displayed on each level. All had some aspect of pink or purple frosting.

A spray of early lilacs in a milky white vase was the centre piece. Strawberries sliced to imitate hearts were placed on tiny purple-iced cupcakes. Crust-less cucumber sandwiches were stacked high on a white and purple china plater. Smaller plates were ready to use for the food, next to a fan of gleaming sterling-silver flatware. Gladys had to hand it to her. Enid set a pretty tea table.

"This looks lovely, Enid." Gladys said. She moved her notebook from her lap and tucked it beside her. It would be tea first, before all else, then the meeting could begin.

"Thank you, I'll pour the tea and then you can help yourselves." Enid was flushed with pleasure at the praise.

Just as Enid picked up the shiny teapot and a delicate china cup and saucer, the hallway door opened again without preamble. Dwayne Davis walked in like he owned the place.

With no apology, the condo president strutted over to them. He gave the tea and all the fixings a flat look. "Have you got a beer, Enid?"

"Yes, of course, one minute." Enid moved the tea strainer to the next cup. "Will you take over, Gladys?" Without waiting for an answer, she put the pot down on the trolley and turned the handled toward Gladys and then hurried off back to the kitchen.

Dwayne leaned down and used one beefy finger to turn the pot in a circle, letting the light glint off the rich antique finish. Then he grunted and moved away.

For her part, Gladys handed the full teacup with saucer to Linda who waved off the offer of milk, sugar, and lemon.

"Tea, Freddie?"

"Yeah, I guess."

Gladys poured three more cups. Hers, she only filled a third of the way. Then exchanged the tea for the hot water pot on the trolley and brought the level in her cup to half an inch from the gold rim. It was unlikely the tea was decaffeinated. A cup of tea at full strength at this time in the evening would have Gladys wide awake well into the wee hours.

Enid returned with a frosty mug containing at least ten ounces of a straw-coloured brew. She placed a coaster on the purple wooden table and put the glass mug on top.

Dwayne merely nodded, like it was his due, and did not thank his hostess. Still, she gave Dwayne a fond smile and moved to perch on the couch.

"Have you started yet?" Dwayne asked, picking up his drink.

"No, not yet, but we can now you are here." Enid picked up a plate of sandwiches to hand around.

The board president fished in his front right pocket and extracted a gold pocket watch and opened it. He glanced at the time and snapped it closed and then made another noise between a grunt and a sigh. "We're burning day light."

Linda paused in handing out serviettes and narrowed her eyes at Dwayne. Gladys ignored Dwayne's presidentially bossy tone. Nothing would be accomplished by pointing out he was merely board president until the next election. Dwayne would merely smirk at her.

Freddie looked into the depths of his tea as Enid offered him a sandwich. Gladys thought her neighbour had the look of a man who would have preferred a beer too, instead of tea. However, Freddie politely took a sandwich and cupcake, and thanked their hostess. He put them on a small plate and balanced it on his knee.

"All right then, we should get going." Enid called the meeting to order.

There was a requirement to review the minutes from the last meeting including the damage report and repair breakdown from the contractors hired to replace the damaged drywall, flooring, and wood trim in Linda's and Dwayne's apartments, the hallway, and the ceiling in Dwayne's condo, among other things.

"Now, the previous work will probably all have to all be redone." Enid pursed her lips at Linda. "Of course, this time there will be additional charges due to the damage to the elevator and the parking garage. The floors might need to be replaced there, too."

Linda flushed in embarrassment and dropped her eyes to the teacup she clutched.

Gladys doubted Enid's words. The whole bottom level of the building was concrete. There hadn't been that much water. She opened her mouth to say exactly that, but Freddie beat her to it.

"As far as I can tell, there were only wet rugs, which were taken care of with the steam cleaner Linda rented. Linda made quick work of that water, with some help from Gladys earlier." He gave each woman a nod in turn. "There was nowhere near the water this time as there was from the ruptured water heater. Not even as much as when Linda's dishwasher blew that hose connection." He gestured to Enid with his cake fork. "I don't think it will be necessary to require a third special assessment."

"We haven't had the elevator inspected yet. We don't know." Enid countered.

"Exactly, we don't know," Gladys said. "I don't agree we should request or surrender another large lump sum until we know if there is any damage. Not without an estimate and only after the work is completed."

"She's accusing you of jumping the gun, Enid." Dwayne took a long sip from his beer. A slice of foam stuck to his top lip. "Look, I don't have time for this chit chat. Let's get to the agenda."

"We have to vote on the minutes to be accepted," Enid said, a stickler for procedure.

Dwayne shook his head. "Just table them for now."

Gladys lifted one shoulder. "All right, fine by me." As long as no one expected her to get out her cheque book.

Enid picked up her copy of the agenda. "Let me remind you all what's listed for discussion." She cleared her throat. "Building Water damage," she tossed another narrow-eyed look at Linda. The other woman hid behind her teacup again and kept her eyes down.

"Building security," the manager continued. "Running businesses from residences, pets, special assessment #3, the Airbnb prohibition, and Cannabis." She lowered the paper to her file folders on the side table next to her.

"What about cannabis?" Freddie frowned at the manager.

Enid gave Freddie a stiff smile. "We've had complaints. Lots of them."

"Yeah, all from Lara, the killjoy. I have a medical certificate for my weed. I am well inside the federal law and building bylaws. You can't touch me or my plants." Freddie stated emphatically.

Dwayne narrowed his eyes at Freddie and a smug smile curved his lined face. "We'll see about that."

"I move item one and item five be tabled for now. We don't have all the facts, as Gladys said." Linda interjected.

"It doesn't matter anyway because you are paying for your mess. All of it." Dwayne said emphatically. The smile he gave Linda turned snarky. "There's no way in hell I am." As condo board president, Dwayne had a small side table next to him, on the right. Enid always had placed it there for his portfolio. He now opened the vinyl folder and made notes. His scrawl was in some kind of strange shorthand Gladys had never seen before. Of course, maybe it was his terrible handwriting which made the scrawl look like shorthand. "We'll circle back later to the building security item as well."

"That works for me. So, what is this item about running a home business?" For Gladys this was the most pressing issue next to the 'Pets' item.

"We've had complaints from other residents." Enid said this primly.

"We're going to vote on allowing condo owners to conduct businesses from their residences." Dwayne leveled a hard look at Gladys.

"I so move." Enid jumped in.

"Seconded." This from Dwayne. "All in favour of prohibiting small business from condo units raise your hands." Dwayne looked at Enid.

"I so vote to prohibit, and so too does Lara, I have her proxy." Enid waved a slip of white paper she extracted from a manila tab folder. "I also hold the proxy from Pink Brick." She held up an additional paper. "So that's four votes to prohibit." She smiled expectantly at Dwayne and waited.

He looked steadily back at her. "No, that's three."

Was Dwayne going to abstain, or merely wait to see if his vote was needed? What was he playing at?

"Fine, how many in favour of allowing home-based businesses?" Gladys said quickly.

Linda and Freddie raised their right hands in support of Gladys as she raised hers. She slid her hand into the flap of her portfolio to extract Matthew's email. At worst this vote would end in a tie.

Dwayne turned to look at Enid just as Gladys was unfolding the printed paper. He slowly raised his hand to vote along with the other three. A wicked smile curved his lips.

Enid was out gunned. She aimed her shocked scowl at Dwayne, and he laughed back at her. It wasn't a nice laugh. "I run a small business too. I'm not going to let you ruin it for some petty reason or grudge you have against Gladys."

Gladys quickly recorded the results. "Motion defeated," she said crisply.

The building manager flattened her lips into a straight line and lifted her chin. "Fine." Enid turned her icy stare back to Dwayne. She stretched out her hand, palm up. "Hand over your garage door key fob." It was a clear order.

Gladys took a sip of her tea as she watched the power struggle. Her eyes, like Linda and Freddie moved back and forth between the two combatants as they spoke. She'd won the vote and that was all that mattered.

"Now you're being unreasonable, Enid." Dwayne put down his beer mug and leaned back in the chair as he considered the other woman. His demeaning tone made Gladys grit her teeth.

"You haven't paid the fifty-dollar deposit required to use the fob. Nor have you paid for your parking space in the garage for the past two months. Hand it over." Enid's eyes had gone all flinty.

"Enid," Dwayne poured oily charm into his tone. "I'm sure we can come to some agreement about this. I'm a bit short at the moment. What with the reconstruction in my apartment. I'm sure you understand." He leaned toward her and placed a hand on her knee.

Enid's cheeks flushed to a delicate pink. "I don't know, maybe–"

"Well, that's not fair." Linda stepped into the argument. "I can't afford the extra costs either. I have to park outside, so should you Dwayne."

The building manager pushed Dwayne's hand away. Linda had a point and Enid knew it. "The key fob, please."

Dwayne's eyes cut to Linda. His expression turned ugly. "You shouldn't be allowed to live around people. You're a walking disaster. I've hired a lawyer to bring a civil suit against you, Linda. He'll be serving the papers on you this week. You'd better find the money to pay for all the trouble you cause, because by the time I'm done with you, you'll have to sell out and move." The condo president stood up and dug out his keys. "But don't worry. You can offer to settle if you like, it might be cheaper for you in the long run."

He ripped the fob off the ring and slammed it down on the table making the china cups jump with a clatter. The force of the impact left a small, round indent in the wood. "There you go, Enid." Dwayne bared his teeth at her and stalked out of the living room and through the hallway door, slamming it behind him.

There was a moment or two of awkward silence. Linda was white as a sheet. No doubt from being singled out to receive the brunt of Dwayne's anger. She wasn't the type to handle confrontations well. Neither was Gladys, so she leaned over to pat the younger woman's shoulder. "Don't let it bother you. It was good you spoke your mind."

Mutely, Linda shook her head.

Enid rose smoothly to her feet and snatched up Dwayne's key fob. She said nothing as she walked over her utility room, opened the door, and placed the key fob inside the metal box which housed the building's spare keys.

Gladys noted a single tear wet Enid's cheek as she returned to her seat. It was quickly dashed away.

With one hand Gladys picked up a purple-frosted cupcake and peeled back the paper. "What's this about pets?" She asked.

Matthew's proxy email rested on her folder. She had a feeling the rest of the issues that touched her were going to be decided quickly and in her favour.

Chapter Fourteen

Gladys was up early as per usual the next morning. It was the beginning of another fair-weather day and she was on the hunt.

Even before she had prepared scrambled eggs on sourdough toast for herself and Maisy, the phone had rung.

She'd glanced at the display before sticking the device between her shoulder and ear while she cut orange slices to add to their breakfast. "Hello, Mrs. Roque, what can I do for you?" she said cheerfully and tried to keep the burgeoning hope out of her tone. It wasn't dignified to sound too eager. Mrs. Roque was the manager of Highmere House and Estate. Calls from her meant work was coming, very lucrative work.

"I need a few dozen of your amazing dinner rolls, Gladys."

A wide smile bloomed on Gladys' face.

"I also need a wide variety of dainties."

The smile slid off. "Yes, sure, no problem."

After agreeing to Mrs. Roque's requests, Gladys realized she'd have to find out where she'd put her cookbooks. The move had jumbled her recollection of which, of the still packed containers held the items she needed.

Gladys had used durable tough totes as packing boxes for her move. Partly because she was not sure how many would have to be kept in her storage locker on the parking level. It was not easy to move from a three-bedroom house to an apartment.

In the spare bedroom she checked two containers and moved on to another large blue plastic tote and removed the lid. She shook her head as she sorted through this third box marked 'kitchen'.

A firm knock on her door drew her attention. Briskly she walked out to the foyer and found Arlie standing outside her door. He looked freshly shaved and was neatly dressed in a short-sleeved navy golf shirt and khaki-coloured trousers and brown deck shoes.

Immediately Gladys was conscious of her frumpy loose T-shirt with a faded gecko on the front and her baggy jean shorts. At least she'd washed her face and combed her hair this morning, so that was something. "Hi, what's going on?"

"Nothing, I just wanted to drop by."

"Come in, you can give me a hand, if you don't mind."

A grin split Arlie's seamed face. "Absolutely.

Now Gladys and Arlie were standing in the spare bedroom of her condo. But that was okay. Even though there was a bed and dresser in the room, it wasn't really a bedroom. She used the space as a storage room. Of course, Sunday she'd have to reorganize when Maisy came back.

"What are you up to?" Arlie looked around at the haphazardly stacked totes.

"I'm looking for some cookbooks. Those are the ones, I've checked." She gestured to the two stacked under the window. "I've moved on to this one."

Arlie nodded. "You want all the ones marked 'kitchen' then."

"Yes, please." She turned back to the open container.

"I thought we'd done a neater job than this." Arlie found another kitchen tote and put it beside Gladys.

She frowned into the third container she'd search. "I can't believe how tossed about all my stuff is. I thought these totes would protect the packed items better."

"Have you sorted through them before this, looking for something?"

"No, when have I had time? My baking business is taking off, I'm crazy busy. If this keeps up, I'll have to hire help or something." She dug to the bottom of the tote. "Nope, no cookbooks in this one either."

Arlie replaced the lid and stacked the tote on top of the previous ones. "You can't have that many kitchen totes. Your cookbooks have to be here somewhere."

"You'd be surprised." She moved on to the next container. Working as a team, Arlie popped open the lid for her. "Geez, this one is a real mess." Kitchen knickknacks she now wished she'd sold or given away took up most of box. She dug down among the paper wrapped ceramic figurines and wall plates. "Ha, I feel a book. Yep, they're in here." She gently extracted three cookbooks. "These will do."

"Why do you need cookbooks anyway?" Arlie moved about the room bringing order to the brown and blue containers. He arranged them with the labels turned out and left space between the rows for Gladys to move between them.

"Mrs. Roque called me about baking for the Music and Literature Society fundraising dinner. Supplying ten dozen dinner rolls is a piece of cake, but it's the small cakes and dainties that are the problem. She wants fancy, and it's been an age since I've done those. Really, I wished she'd called Jane."

"Ah, I know why," Arlie said. He looked down as he reattached the brown plastic lid onto a container.

"Why?"

"Jane's Eats and Treats is catering the Society's dinner. That's one of the reasons why I dropped by."

Gladys nodded. "It's this Saturday. You have to cancel on the dinner party."

"Yep, sorry about this. Plus, we need Maisy to serve too. There's too much to do for just me and Jane. Jack has been enlisted too." Arlie's mouth curved into a mischievous smile. "I don't think he knows yet."

"Will that be a problem?"

"Heh, no, my son will do anything to help his wife, and vice versa. Sorry about dinner."

"Don't worry about it. I was going to ask you and Jane if you'd mind if I postponed anyway." Gladys waved a hand at him to let him know there was no problem with this change in plans. She lifted her eyebrows at him in question. "Do you need my help?"

"That might be an idea." Arlie nodded. "Mrs. Roque said she has a hundred and fifty attending the banquet. I bet we could use all the help we can get."

"Talk to Jane and let me know." Her forehead creased into a frown. "If those are the numbers, ten dozen isn't going to be nearly enough. I'll have to give Mrs. Roque a call."

Gladys' eye fell on a dark blue plastic container stacked at the bottom of a pile of three. From the shorthand she'd used to label the contents with a black marker, it was easy to know what was inside this box. "I want to open this one. It's that last one, I promise."

Arlie gave her an indulgent smile. "No problem." He efficiently moved the totes around for her and popped off the lid.

The contents of this box were also jumble. The blank cream-coloured newsprint had been pulled off and pushed to one side. It was as if the items had been dumped unceremoniously into the tote.

A dark feeling crept up Gladys' spine. "Oh, no." She whispered, and reached in among the crumpled packing paper, pushing it aside. Tentatively, she lifted out an eight-by-twelve square wooden box and set it on the bed and ran her hand over the lid.

"What's wrong, Gladys?"

She shook her head wordlessly and opened the mahogany jewelry box's lid. Her carefully stored keepsakes were topsy-turvy. Necklaces where hopelessly tangled. These were costume jewelry pieces she acquired over the years but not her main concern. She slid open a drawer on the left side and looked in. A gold man's wedding ring should have glinted back at her, but there was nothing. Biting her bottom lip, she slid the drawer closed and opened another, then another. All were empty.

Gladys pushed back her rising panic as she straightened to look at Arlie. "Would you mind taking the books to the kitchen, please? The coffee should be ready by now."

"Sure." Arlie said uncertainly. He took the cookbooks and followed Gladys out of the small room. He went through to the living room, and she went to her bedroom.

She placed the box Micky had made for her, almost forty years ago, on top of her dresser. One piece of paper was still lodged into the bottom drawer which was as large as the box's footprint. Gladys knew what she would find, still she had to look.

Using the tiny black stainless-steel handles Micky had forged for the box, she opened the drawer. All that was left inside was the red velvet lining. Micky's silver coin collection was gone.

Gladys gently slid the wooden drawer closed. Then another thought occurred to her, and she quickly returned to the spare room. There was nothing on the spare bed but pillows. Maisy's electronic keyboard was gone too.

She went out to the kitchen and slumped down in one chair.

"What's wrong?" Arlie pushed a mug her way.

"I've been robbed."

Chapter Fifteen

Later that afternoon, with a rack of multigrain loaves in her hands, Gladys aimed one round hip at the crossbar on the back door of her building. Surprisingly, she met no resistance and stumbled. The rack was jolted from her grasp when it hit the door frame.

"I got it." The bread and rack were rescued from falling to the ground by Arlie.

Gladys looked up with a startled expression. "I didn't see you there when I pushed the door handle."

Sheepishly, Arlie adjusted his hold on the rack, trying not to squish any loaves. "Sorry, I should have waited a tick."

She steadied herself on the doorjamb. "I'm just glad you're back from town. You've got quick reflexes, thank you."

Arlie shrugged awkwardly. "I'll take this to your car."

Gladys gave him a grateful smile. Was that a blush on his cheeks?

"Thanks, I'll go get another one. The back gate of the wagon is unlocked."

Five minutes later, Arlie and Gladys had her car loaded. "Did the cops come and see you yet?" He nudged the last rack inside past the door frame.

Fishing the car keys out of her front pocket, Gladys shook her head. "Tomorrow morning is the earliest they can get someone to come and speak to me. I could drive into Duncan or Ganges and make a statement, but I'm too busy." She knew she sounded defeated. That was exactly how she felt and didn't like it. "I should have looked in the totes two days ago. I thought someone had gotten into my condo. Now there's nothing for the RCMP to fingerprint. How will they ever get Micky's things back anyway? It's too easy to sell off gold and silver."

"No, don't say that." Arlie didn't offer any empty platitudes, and for that Gladys was grateful. "I don't like the sound of you giving up. You're stronger than that."

Breathing in deep through her nose, she straightened her shoulders. "You're right. I need to think positive until I know different." She'd make the effort to get a grip. Maisy needed to be told about her keyboard too. Gladys hoped finding out about her grandmother's break-in wouldn't freak the girl out. Then something else occurred to her, "The robbery does explain one thing at least."

"What's that?"

"How a trapdoor spider got into my living room."

"Eeew." He wrinkled his nose.

Gladys laughed as she was meant to, but genuinely appreciated Arlie's attempts to cheer her up. "That's what Maisy said when she saw it too."

"Hi there, Gladys, Arlie." A voice called over.

The pair glanced up and saw Freddie. He was walking through the parking lot past them and lifted a hand.

"Hi, Freddie." Gladys waved at her neighbour. She elbowed Arlie and he gave the other man a brief wave too. Her neighbour grinned and strolled inside the building.

Arlie stepped back from Gladys' car and closed the heavy tailgate of the station wagon. His hand paused on the chrome door handle. For a moment he looked at the station wagon with a pensive frown. "I keep meaning to ask, wasn't this Earl Moffatt's old hearse?"

Gladys knew what Arlie was doing. He was trying to distract her from thinking about being robbed, and she could have hugged him for the effort, so she played along. "Yes, I got it at a good price. The rollers make moving the bread racks so much easier." She patted the side of the car.

"That they do. I don't know why I never realized that before. I've seen this wagon many times since Sara passed."

Gladys watched her friend for a moment. "Micky took his last ride in this vehicle too." She rubbed a smudge off the window with the sleeve of her sweater. Late afternoon was bringing a cool breeze with it. "Do you feel weird about me using an old hearse as a bakery delivery vehicle?"

"No," Arlie said slowly. He turned to look at her. "It's just—"

The navy-blue plumbing van pulled away from the side of the road and sped down the access from the street to the condo parking lot. The vehicle came to an abrupt halt in the middle of the open space between the cars. The back doors flew open. Police officers, dressed in black tactical gear and RCMP emblazoned on their vests, sprang out of the back of the van.

Automatically, Gladys and Arlie moved behind her car, using it as a shield.

"I don't think this is about your robbery, Gladys." Arlie put an arm around her shoulders.

"I don't think so either. Those guys are equipped for trouble. What the heck is going on?" Gladys watched wide-eyed.

"Looks like a bust of some kind." Arlie moved them further back from the action.

Weapons held tight across their chests, muzzle down, two cops, one male, and one female, jogged around to the front of the building. From the angle where she stood, Gladys could see one officer take a position at the entrance. Two more positioned themselves at the garage door.

Two males and one female lined up at the back door. Weapons raise upward, at a safe angle, left hand resting on the shoulder of the person in front, they entered the building quickly, single file.

"We should back up to the road," Arlie suggested. "Just in case."

"Who could they be after? Which of my neighbours is a criminal and bad enough to rate this kind of thing?" Gladys sputtered, but she allowed him to take her hand and lead the way down the drive and up the small rise to Coast Road. "Who do you think they're after?"

"I'm hoping it's Lara Finkle."

"Arlie, really?" Gladys gave him a sharp look.

He shrugged. "We'll just have to watch and see." There was excitement in his tone. Gladys rolled her eyes, but still took a spot beside him which afforded them a view of the back entrance.

A crash drew their attention to a second-floor balcony. The glass balcony doors were open and potted plants were being hurled, one after the other, over the railing and landing on the sidewalk like moist missiles. Multi-coloured plastic cracked and spilled the plants and dirt out on the condo grounds.

Arlie and Gladys exchanged a look. "Freddie." They both said at the same time."

"Somehow, I'm not surprised." Arlie added.

Gladys crossed her arms over her middle. "This is terrible. How could he get himself into so much trouble?"

"I don't know, but to get this kind of a response from the authorities, it's serious. Don't feel too sorry for Freddie."

Norm Gorlitz charged out from behind his garden shed. "What the hell is going on?". He was carrying his garden claw and a plastic lawn bag of hog weed he must have been removing from the rose patches.

"Norm, come away from there." Arlie called out.

The other man turned to them but waved his tool at the plants being lobbed over the balcony. "This is criminal!" It was possible Norm couldn't see the police van that rolled up behind the plumbing van.

"Yes, it is, but come out of the way. Let the police handle it." Gladys urged, gesturing for her friend to come over to them.

Slowly Norm, walked parallel to the building, only now seeing the cops and the police vehicles. He blinked in surprise, and his mouth hung open, trying to form words.

"Norm, seriously come this way." Arlie's voice seemed to penetrate, and the gardener walked over to them, still clutching his bag full of hog weed and the garden claw. "I can't believe what Freddie's done. That's so cruel."

"I'm sure there's no lasting damage. You can wait here with us. We should know the outcome soon." Gladys patted Norm's arm.

They didn't have long to wait. First, the couple who were staying at the new Airbnb burst out of the back door. The young man was missing his shirt and the woman was barefoot. They spotted the seniors and ran up the driveway to where Gladys and Arlie stood.

Two more pots were launched from the balcony.

The young man was wide-eyed. "What is going on? The cops told us to leave."

Eagerly, Arlie supplied the information. "It's a drug bust."

The girl turned to them. "I thought this would be a nice quiet place to stay. Old people are usually so calm and, and boring." Her words stumbled out.

Arlie's face puckered at her remark. "We weren't always old, you know. And just because we are old doesn't mean we don't have anything going on."

"Apparently not," Gladys said dryly to Arlie. She then turned to the younger woman. "I understand how you feel." Gladys gave the girl a bright smile. "Don't judge us all the same though."

Arlie snorted. "They're coming out. I guess it's over."

The other heads swirled to watch the scene. Freddie Freeman was being escorted out the back door. The second-floor resident was handcuffed, but the police officers posture was much more relaxed.

One male was stowing weapons in the back of the 'plumbing van'.

"Let's find out what's going on." Arlie strode forward.

Gladys sighed and trailed after her friend.

Norm followed too. "I hope they throw the book at him."

Freddie was yelling. "I'm allowed five plants by law, Constable Tadmore."

"I know Mr. Freeman, but you have way more than five. Please stop shouting."

"Thirty-five is excessive, sir," one of the female cops said with the blonde ponytail protruding from under her helmet. She walked past Freddie and unclipped her radio mic. "We're clear here at 636 Coast Road, bring in the cleanup crew. We also need transport for one."

So, that was Maisy's Constable Tadmore. He was tall, dark, and handsome, and very fit. No wonder Maisy appeared to have an instant crush on him. Gladys watched the young man bring Freddie along with interest.

"Those other plants, most are donations. Rescues, really. They aren't mine. "

"Not yours? I see, then who do the plants actually belong to?" Tadmore sounded skeptical, and yet slowed their walk to police vehicle.

"Friends and friends of friends. I was only nursing them back to health." Freddie sounded more than a touch desperate. "I was only taking care of the plants until they were better, honest. Most people don't know how to care for these types of plants properly. The poor things were on death's door before I took them in. I saved them." Freddie said self-righteously with an emphatic nod.

"If that's true, why did you throw a bunch of them off your balcony?" The blonde cop gave Freddie a level look. Her tone fetched him up.

"I...um." Freddie dropped his chin.

"You give me the names of your friends and we'll look into it." Tadmore said.

Freddie lifted his chin, surprised. "You will?"

"Of course." He gave Freddie a sunny smile. "It will help your case if your friends claim their property."

"Oh, okay."

HALF AN HOUR LATER, the residents were all allowed back into the building. Gladys decided to check on Albert and Blofeld before she left to make her deliveries, what with all the craziness of the past hour.

Dwayne exited his apartment and looked like he wanted to avoid everyone as he elbowed his way through them to the back door.

Then the elevator bell pinged. "When the hell was the elevator unlocked? I've been using the stair." Dwayne turned sharply as the doors opened and he all but sprinted over when he saw the new arrival. "Lara," he said with a breathy laugh. "I'm glad you're back."

Arlie and Gladys shared a look as she gave him the key to Matthew's apartment to check on Albert.

Lara Finkle stepped off the elevator. She was dressed in a white linen suit with lots of cleavage and an extra-large black faux pearl necklace. She pursed her lips as she looked Dwayne up and down. Then raised her left arm so her vermilion-red purse slid to the crook of her elbow and stepped off the car in four-inch matching red pumps.

He sidled closer. Dwayne's whole demeanour changed as he approached the other woman and blocked her way by leaning on the wall beside the elevator call buttons with one wide hand.

"Hey, I thought the elevator was out of order." The ginger-haired young woman from the second floor Airbnb pointed out. Her partner followed her back into the building. She pointed to the sign above the call buttons. "I've been using the stairs all this time." She didn't sound happy.

"Oh, Lovey, it's only one flight." The young man slipped an arm around her and moved her along to the stairwell.

"Move, Dwayne I don't have time for your stupid antics today." Lara flicked a hand at him, totally confident she would be obeyed.

Dwayne looked sheepish and stepped back to allow Lara to get by. Her eyes fell on the young the couple. "There's nothing wrong with the elevator, Enid is just over cautious. Enjoy your stay." She said simply, and then dismissed them.

"Lara, do you know what's been going on here?" Dwayne's voice held a lighter tone as he tried to engage the woman in conversation.

Gladys lifted her eyebrows. She watched as Dwayne flash Lara a charming smile and shook her head as she dug out her own apartment keys.

The other woman held up one hand for Dwayne to stop. "I know all about the flood. Not my concern, it's the insurance company's problem. I saw Freddie get arrested just now. That's made my day. Now, get out of my way, Dwayne. I have places to be before you ruin my good mood." Lara dismissed him.

At that moment Vinny Norquay strolled into the foyer. He was much better dressed in a pressed white cotton shirt and navy trousers with sharp creases and his black shoes were polished. He was also cleanly shaven, and the scent of male cologne cleaved through the air. "Are you ready, Lara?"

"I am, thanks Vinny." She reached out one hand and Vinny took it, all while giving Dwayne a smug look.

The condo board president bared clenched his teeth, but he said nothing.

Gladys slid her key in the deadbolt lock wondering what had happened between Lara and Vinny to put them both on the same side. He must have caught up with her at some point and maybe Lara paid him after all.

"Mrs. Wyatt?"

Gladys turned to see who addressed her. It was the RCMP officer who'd arrested Freddie.

"I'm Constable Tadmore, you reported a break and enter earlier today?"

"I did, yes."

"Can we take your statement now?"

"Yes, absolutely, would you like to come in?" Gladys gestured to her unit.

"I would, thanks, this shouldn't take too long."

Lara pulled her hand from Vinny's to stalk across the foyer and up to Tadmore. "Wait a minute. What about my report? Where are my things? You need to–" She made a movement to stick her finger in his chest, but the constable nimbly performed a sidestep before she could touch him.

"Please, don't touch me, Ms. Finkle." There was a definite warning in Tadmore's voice.

"Lara, don't be rude to the Constable." Gladys frowned at the other woman.

The cop lifted his hands in a wait gesture to Lara. "We are working on your case as well, Ms. Finkle. Mrs. Wyatt's burglary is probably connected to yours. So, excuse me, I need to take her statement."

Arlie walked over and slipped behind the group to the condo door and held it open for them. The cop and Gladys walked past him entered the ground floor apartment. Just before Arlie allowed the door close, Gladys spied an obviously miffed Lara stalking out the front entrance with Vinny trailing behind her.

Dwayne Davis had already slipped away. Gladys wondered if he was fuming at being jilted.

Once inside, Gladys led the constable to the living room and offered him a seat. "Can I get you anything? Coffee, tea, water?"

"No thank you, ma'am. I have to go with my team back to the Detachment as soon as I'm done here." He took out an occurrence note pad and pen from his side trouser pocket and sat down. "I thought I'd drop by after...after the other call."

Gladys snorted. "You mean the drug bust? That was quite exciting for this sleepy village."

"Not so sleepy with these burglaries, and the shenanigans at the pump house." The constable tipped his head slightly to one side as he looked back at her.

"That's certainly true." Arlie nodded, rocking back on his heals with his hands in his jean pockets.

Her friend was striving to look wide-eyed and innocent. Gladys gave him a withering look as she sat across from the officer.

"What?" Arlie asked with a grin.

"You are such an instigator. Don't you have anything to do?" Gladys asked.

"Yep, I do. Can I catch up with you later?"

"Yes, of course. Thanks for your help loading the car."

"No problem." Arlie briefly rested a hand on her shoulder and then he was gone.

"Was your husband not around when the theft took place?"

"Arlie Birch isn't my husband, just a friend. My husband passed away several years ago. It was his wedding band which was stolen, along with his silver dollar collection."

"So that's Arlie Birch." Tadmore allowed a half smile.

"That's him all right, who brought him to your attention?"

"Your mayor, Ann Westcott. I need to speak to him and you too, about these banners on the pump house."

Gladys mimicked Arlie's innocent expression. "Oh? About what?" she asked in a gentle voice.

"First, let's talk about the items which were stolen."

"Yes." Gladys sobered. "I think all the contents of my storage containers were rifled through, but I don't have much of value. Unfortunately, the thief found the little I did have." A thought struck her. "Are you going to check for fingerprints?"

"We are, but don't get your hopes up. The other break-ins left no evidence, the perpetrator used gloves."

"I'm sorry to hear that." Gladys' mouth turned down. "My granddaughter's keyboard is missing too."

Chapter Sixteen

Thursday afternoon turned warmer as Gladys drove her car loaded with bread and rolls out of the village. If she traveled north from the hamlet of Whisky Corner, she could hook up with the new road which traveled over the mountains to Fulsome Harbour some fifty kilometres away.

Along that route were a scattering of acreages. Some posh homes close the beach and the rest farther inland with folks who like to keep to themselves. These were some of her regular customers.

They liked the convenience of meeting her at the crossroad to collect their bread orders and not having to travel into Musgrave Landing for the diet staple. This cluster of islanders liked their privacy. The acreages all had gardens and most kept animals and chickens, so their trips into the village proper were less often and much less necessary.

Last was the trip to the Smuggler's Inn. Gladys liked to leave Casey's Inn for last so she could take a break before making the drive home.

She turned right again to follow the less well-maintained route beyond Whisky Corner. She wasn't two minutes on the narrow track that passed for a road when her right front tire found a pothole and splashed the front end of her car and windshield with dirty water.

Gladys sighed with resignation. The simulated wood panelling always got muddy on these trips. It was the price of doing business with the locals and the Smuggler's Inn.

Even though the hamlet of Whiskey Corner was merely a collection of houses clustered around an intersection which led south, and down the rocks to Brown's Beach, it was worth the trip. Even more so than the mariner's market.

The Inn was one of her best customers, with Casey requiring a dozen loaves of multi-grain and a dozen flax seed, and half a dozen of white. Then of course the extra-large rolls the innkeeper and chef used to serve either with seafood chowder or as the actual bowl for his hearty beef stew or chili.

"When are you going to offer me some gluten free baking?" The big burly man asked her as he looked over his invoice.

His blond-red beard covered a good portion of his face making his expression hard to discern, but his question had given Gladys pause all the same. "Are you serious or is this more of your twisted sense of humour?"

"Well." And he'd drawn out the word. "All right you have me there. I'm just pullin' your leg." He opened a leather-bound business cheque book and filled in the amounts and signed the payment.

Gladys accepted the stiff paper and folded it neatly to tuck into her wallet. "I thought so. Still, is there much demand for gluten free bread? I guess I could try making some." In her head, she rapidly calculated the cost and effort of making a limited run of gluten-free products.

"Oh, yeah, once a week or so. I keep some store bought in the freezer for those people." He put his cheque book away in the desk drawer.

"It wouldn't be cheap. I'd have to charge half again more than a regular loaf of flax seed or multigrain. Rice flour is expensive and harder to work with. This is the first time anyone's asked for it."

Casey waved a massive hand in a never mind gesture. "Don't worry about it. I get asked more for vegan bread anyway."

Gladys shook her head in confusion. "Isn't most bread vegan already?"

"From what I'm told by my customers, no, apparently not," Casey said with a shrug. "I know yours qualifies because you'd tell me if you put any animal products into the dough."

"Yes, I would. The cost would go up if I used milk instead of water too. The rest is flour, canola oil, seeds, yeast, sugar to make it rise, salt to kill the rise, and that's all. Same as it's printed on the labels stuck to the bags." Gladys could not help that her tone was a bit firmer than necessary. She was somewhat hurt at having her craft questioned.

Casey must have sensed her feelings. He raised both of his big hands in a placating gesture. "And darn tasty your bread is too. I'd never buy from anyone else, not while you are in business."

"Thank you," she said, mollified.

"Come in for some lemonade or ice tea. I have something I want to run past ya."

Gladys raised her eyebrows, curious. She followed Casey from the huge, well-appointed kitchen to the bar in the main part of the two-hundred-year-old converted farmhouse.

Varnished cedar beams and trim contrasted well with the forest green paint on the walls. Matching green fabric was used for the over-stuffed chairs which were scattered around like a sitting room. Low tables were placed among the chairs and in front of the huge patio doors which led to a wraparound veranda. These allowed guests to sit comfortably inside and enjoy the ocean across the road. They could also go outside to sit on an old-fashioned wooden swing or use the Adirondack chairs placed on the veranda in pairs. The tide was in, so no trace of the rugged black rocks could be seen at the moment. Only the shifting and glinting waters of the Strait of Juan de Fuca sliding gently over the large mass of stones.

Casey went behind the bar. A two-foot by four-foot double sided bookcase was converted to a counter/bar area, also made from the red cedar wood with two bar stools placed in front. The books were still kept on the shelves and Gladys could imagine guests selecting one and taking a seat in front of the fireplace on the north wall.

Gladys clambered up on one of the bar stools. Once seated, she realized she was actually thirsty.

What was once the dining room for the farmhouse now held a stainless-steel fridge, wine storage, and hanging rack for glasses of various sizes. Behind the counter, were three beer taps. The first two offered two regular commercial brands and the third was 'Casey's Own Select'.

Up on the highest shelf which ran along the ceiling, Casey displayed his collection of vintage hard liquor bottles and polished copper vessels. These alluded to the Inn's past.

Whisky Corner got its name from a time in the 1920's, after British Columbia reversed its policy on prohibition. The law was still in force next door in Washington State well into the 1930's. Even though American residents of that state could obtain some forms of liquor for medicinal purposes, commercial spirits were not available.

This opportunity led the local fishermen to get involved in alcohol smuggling. Hence the name of Casey's Inn. A short trot down the road out front, took one to the beach and the caves used for storage of the brews.

Fishing for prawns and crab took boats over the water boundary between the two countries on a daily basis. It was fairly easy to organize exchanges.

The Smuggler's Inn detailed the colourful prohibition history of the area. The information was compiled in the pamphlets and a book for sale from a local author who had written about the history. This made an entertaining narrative for the tourists. Along with Casey's excellent meals, he served large pints of his own microbrewery beer, and wine, but no hard stuff.

"So, what's up?" Gladys watched Casey remove a large picture of lemonade from the glass-front fridge. He added ice to a couple of glasses.

"You're part of the Musgrave Landing Players, aren't you?"

"Yes, we did 'Murder Inn the Family' for this past spring's dinner theatre."

"I know, Ivy and I saw the Saturday evening performance. Great roast beef by the way." Casey poured the drinks and placed Gladys' on the coaster in front of her.

"I'll tell Jane you said so."

"Oh, you guys were good too. Sorry, I should have said." Casey sounded a bit flummoxed.

Why was he nervous? "Thank you. We had fun and like to help out local charities with the proceeds."

"Would you like to do if for money? Acting, I mean."

"Heh, I doubt it."

"Oh." True disappointment was in Casey's single word.

"Why, what are you trying rather badly to get at?"

The man straightened his spine and towered over her. "I want to put on mystery weekends over the winter. At least one to start. Things are slow from mid-January to mid-February. I need something to bring the people out during the six weeks."

"Aren't mystery weekends pretty much done? I haven't heard anyone doing any since the late nineties." She sipped her lemonade, it was perfect. Not over sweet or tart.

He spread his hands. "So, I'll bring them back into style."

"Who's going to write the mysteries? You can't use a full three act play."

"I will, I have, actually. I was thinking of three acts. The Friday is the first act, Saturday, the second and Saturday night the third, where it's all wrapped up. Then the guests leave Sunday morning." His words got faster as he spoke.

Casey was excited, but whether by the prospect of more customers or writing the plays, she didn't know.

"We would keep the cast small. I would use the guests as part of the play. They each have a part with set goals they have to achieve. A clue or red herring they are supposed to share, but they don't know which ahead of time. Only at the end."

"Okay." Gladys nodded. "Sounds interesting. You wanted me to come for the weekend, and participate?"

"Yeah, you and Arlie, maybe one or two more. We'll have to work out the details. Can you ask him for me and let me know? We can figure out the details this summer. Then get together to negotiate payment. Oh, and how we'd work the mystery side of things."

"All right. Sure, I'll mention your idea to Arlie. Kind of sounds like fun."

Chapter Seventeen

Back in Musgrave Landing, Gladys hauled the now empty bread trays out of the back of her station wagon. The sun was low in the sky. This was the time of day she felt her age and wondered why she was working so hard. She rested the three empty racks on her hip and swung the heavy gate of the Ford Country Wagon closed.

This Sunday after church she would have some spare time. With no orders due, after brunch she planned to give the old station wagon a thorough cleaning. As she plodded over to the back entrance, she heard a scream from the side of the building. Startled, Gladys came to a stop and turned toward the driveway which led to the basement level parking.

"Help! Someone help me!" Came the agonizing cry.

Instinctively fearing the worst, Gladys dropped the racks on the pavement and ran toward the sound of desperate crying. It was a woman in distress.

Not thinking what the cause could be, the sixty-six-year-old galloped rounded the corner of the condo building and came to an abrupt halt at the site.

There, Enid was doubled over, shrieking. She had her hand braced on the side of the building, in front of the sliding garage door. Her other arm was wrapped around her middle as she sobbed. The middle-aged woman sounded like she was in horrible pain.

That was when Gladys saw the cowboy boots sticking out past the concrete pillars which framed the sliding garage door. She recognized those signature boots.

Immediately Gladys ran forward. As she got closer, she knew it was bad. Dwayne must have collapsed. "Enid, is it a heart attack?"

She skidded to a stop and immediately knew this was no heart attack. The large metal door was mostly lowered closed. Dwayne's chest was the only thing holding the door up.

"Oh, my lord!" Hurriedly she scrambled to dig her mobile phone out of her front pocket. With trembling fingers, she stabbed 911.

LATER, GLADYS HARDLY remembered what she'd said to emergency services. Her throat had closed up at the sight of Dwayne lying on the concert ramp. Even as she checked for a pulse, she knew he was dead. There was something so still about a body with no soul in residence.

Now she leaned on the garden wall beside the pink rose bush with Linda and Norm. They were the only other two people currently around building and heard the commotion with the ambulance. They'd both came outside to see what all the fuss was about and stayed to offer support.

The RCMP arrived minutes later and took charge of the scene.

Twenty minutes after that, Freddie ambled up the driveway. He was stopped by a cop, but he gestured to those along the wall and then the condo building. Apparently, explaining he was a resident.

"Can't they move his body?" Linda asked as they all watched Freddie approach.

"Not until the coroner gets here." Gladys shook her head.

"Looks like Freddie's out on bail." Norm said sourly. He sounded like he did not approve. This was confirmed by the dirty look Norm gave him as Freddie sauntered over to the group clustered by one of the planters filled with red roses.

"Hi ya." Freddie looked at them uncertainly and then back at the cluster of vehicles in the condo parking lot. There was a group of people in various uniforms encircling the white ground sheet which obscured the view of Dwayne's body from head to toe.

"Hi, Freddie." Gladys murmured, unable to shift her attention away from the activity.

Linda greeted the other resident. Norm ignored him as he stoically watched the scene in front of them.

After a minute of awkward silence Freddie asked, "Heart attack?"

"It was an accident," Linda said. She had her arms wrapped around herself, rubbing her hands up and down her arms. She also had the same bleak look she always had when a disaster befell the building, like she was two seconds away from bursting into tears.

Gladys felt empathy for Linda and wanted to point out this time the disastrous events weren't her fault, not that it would change anything. Linda's emotions were fairly transparent.

"Accident? Then why are the cops here?" Freddie frowned.

"Hush, Freddie." Gladys said as, she watched a tall, dark-haired female cop offer Enid a bottle of water. Enid pushed it away. The building manager had stopped her wailing and now sat tight lipped, and glassy-eyed in one of the police SUVs with the door open.

Had there been more between Enid and Dwayne than Gladys first thought? She knew there was some kind of relationship but found it confusing the way Dwayne treated the other woman and vice versa.

Then there was the fact that every time Lara was around, Dwayne fell all over himself to suck up to the floozy. The word floozy was something Gladys' mother would have used. Still, it fit. Lara Finkle didn't possess many morals. She and Tim Stanhope had carried on for years, right under his wife, Anita's nose. The whole village knew about the affair now, including Anita.

Many people, including Arlie, still wondered if all the money her old boyfriend had embezzled had been found. Yes, Lara had sold her house, but did she make enough to buy a condo in the pricey modern building? Who knew? Maybe Arlie was right, and Lara had squirreled some of the embezzled money away.

Gladys used all her own house sale money and what was left of Micky's life insurance policy to buy her more modest condo. At the time, she thought her decision was an excellent one. Now, she wasn't so sure.

"This is all too weird." Norm said.

"So many strange things happening lately, it's like Armageddon, I tell you!" Freddie stabbed a boney finger in Gladys' direction, making her blink. "Our building is cursed."

Gladys sighed and gave her head a shake, not answering.

"Stop saying paranoid things," Norn snorted.

"No, what makes you say that, Freddie?" Linda was all for investigating the end of the world.

"We've had floods." Freddie began ticking items off with the fingers on his left hand.

Linda instantly reddened. "Those were accidents. I couldn't help the water heater blowing, or the washing machine leaking."

Gladys looked down at her scuffed running shoes and studiously did not mention the dishwasher.

"Everything happens for a reason." Freddie's voice had grown wobbly with intensity. "And then there's these robberies we've been having all over the village, four of us here have been hit, including me." He ticked his crooked middle finger.

"I didn't know you were robbed." Linda said.

Freddie nodded. "My golf clubs and my iPad were stolen." He paused for a moment, apparently deciding if he should continue. "And my plant fund. I had over five hundred in my mason jar under the sink. It's gone."

"You never reported it, did you?" Norm said in a derisive tone. "I saw the ridiculous amount of cannabis plants the police removed from your apartment. You're a drug dealer and a plant killer." Clearly the latter was the paramount crime.

"Yeah? Well, you're a shit kicker."

"Boys." Gladys snapped. "Stop it."

"It's all right Gladys, I'm not embarrassed by my farming roots. Why would I be? Farming is honest, law-abiding work."

"Just stow your bickering. This is not the time," she told them sharply. "There are more serious matters to worry about right now." Gladys was relieved when both males ceased their nattering and fell silent, even if they did exchange an extra glare.

For several more minutes the group of residents watched the police erect a privacy screen around the body.

Abruptly Linda broke the silence. "I guess it's really five of us. Someone stole my secret cookie jar stash." She had been toying with a red bloom. With her words the flower disintegrated in her fingers, and she looked surprised at what she'd done.

Typical, though Gladys, and then frowned at her reaction. Negative thoughts weren't common for her, nor were they helpful. She should be more charitable, Linda was upset too.

"Linda? What kind of stash?" Freddie sounded intrigued.

Gladys surmised with all his cannabis confiscated he would be on the lookout for more.

Linda reached for another flower. Gladys wanted to stop her from destroying a second bloom, but Norm beat her too it.

"Don't fiddle with my roses, Linda."

"Oh, sorry." She lowered her hand and glanced over at Freddie. "My bingo winnings." Linda's skin flushed dark pink. "I was saving up for a new moped. I had three hundred dollars in my owl cookie jar. It's all gone."

"Oh." Freddie disappointment was heartfelt.

Gladys eyed Linda. The amount of heat contained in her last words made them positively molten.

"Maisy's keyboard is missing. I had hoped she'd taken it with her in Matthew's apartment, but it appears no. It must have been stolen from my place when my things went missing."

Freddie narrowed his eyes and continued. "Then there's Matthew's dog." He ticked another finger. "If Albert caught someone breaking in, he'd raise a ruckus. No doubt the thief wanted to silence him."

"You're saying it had to be the thief who threw the dog from the balcony?" Norm asked the other man.

"Yeah."

"Good Lord," Norm said, shocked.

"Maisy said there is no way Albert could have gotten between the glass panels, he's too big." Gladys nodded, still disturbed at the thief's violence. "How could anyone hurt such a sweet dog?" Gladys was troubled about the thought of some stranger breaking into her home, but worse was anyone, including animals, being hurt. She was lucky Blofeld hadn't been injured.

"What kind of monster would hurt a defenceless puppy?" Linda's outrage was apparent and the other three nodded.

"The unnatural kind," Freddie said knowingly. "A sick and vindictive individual."

"Five minutes in jail, and you understand everything about the criminal mind, do you?" Norm scoffed.

"It was a long five minutes."

Norm snorted, amused this time.

Gladys's lips compressed into a flat line as she considered the robberies and the fact Dwayne had been booted out of the bar at the marina. She was sure Freddie didn't know any more about the thefts than she did, or any of the other condo building residents, but he did have one thing right. There had been a lot of strangeness going on lately and most of it seemed to be centred in their building. There was the distinct possibility Dwayne had been behind some of it.

From the corner of her eye, she caught movement on the street. The coroner's white panel van drove slowly down the driveway. The vehicle came to a stop just outside the yellow and black police caution tape.

"Looks like Enid's calmed down, that's something." Linda jerked her chin toward the building manager. "I bet the cops will want to talk to you next, Gladys."

"I've already spoken to the first officer who arrived, Constable Tadmore. I just made the call. I wasn't here when the door fell on Dwayne." Gladys shuttered involuntarily as the image of Dwayne's cowboy boots sticking out. The rest of him hidden by the corner of the building. Then to see the garage door resting on his chest, she shivered.

She felt a firm hand on her shoulder, patting it. "You might have seen something or someone when you drove up. We don't know it was an accident." Norm moved his hand away and shifted his feet. He transferred his long-handled garden claw into his left hand. There were dark brown stains on the front of his shirt and the dark blue work pants he wore.

His hand left a dark stain on Gladys' top, but she appreciated his support and gave Norm a weak smile in thanks. "This had to be an accident. How else could this be explained?" Gladys couldn't help the tremble in her voice. She cleared her throat to cover it.

"I don't believe in accidents," Freddie told them firmly. "Dwayne was a nasty piece of work. He called the cops on me, I know it."

Gladys looked at him. "Why would he do that? How would Dwayne know you had too many cannabis plants in you unit?"

Freddie gave her a pitying look. "Dwayne is always looking for a quick buck and doesn't care how he gets it."

"And what exactly does that mean?" Norm shook his grey head. "Out with it, stop beating around the bush."

"Dwayne found out I had more than my legally allowed share of plants. I don't know how. Maybe Lara mentioned it, whatever. Anyway, he turned up at my door a couple of weeks ago and threatened to report me if I didn't pay him sixty percent of my sales."

"How much would that be?" Linda asked.

"Nothing, I don't sell the weed. I give it away."

"Really?" Gladys said dubiously. "And Lara is a customer?"

Freddie snorted. "No, but lots of other people are. And I don't charge for the bud. People give me donations when they drop off their plants or pick up their supply." He lifted his hands in a defensive posture. "I can't help it if some people are terrible with plants. I was just trying to help them." He dropped his hands to his sides.

Norm grunted in agreement.

Chapter Eighteen

The four of them watched as Enid was led inside the building by Maude Barber. Maude had artificial russet hair which she currently had tied back in a stubby ponytail. She had the shoulders and arms of a weightlifter. There was nothing lightweight about the woman, so it didn't matter Enid was taller by several inches. As an Emergency Medical Services senior volunteer, Maude was more than capable for the job. She also trained the new recruits. In her other life Maude was a part-time shelf stocker at the B&H Country Grocers store and loved interacting with people. Gladys knew Maude would use any talent at her disposal to shield Enid from any further distress when the body was moved.

A tall male, broad-shouldered Sikh RCMP constable followed behind them. His navy-blue turban made him look even larger. This was the first time Gladys thought Enid looked average size or even small. Like this incident had reduced her somehow.

"If this were a British mystery, I would expect the kettle to be put on and a low-key interview would follow with fortifying tea and a chocolate biscuits," Norm said.

Gladys got to her feet.

"Where are you off to?" Norm slapped his garden gloves against his left thigh.

"I need to let Albert out for a piddle." That was one thing, but also her bottom was going numb from sitting on the concrete planter and it wasn't doing her back any good either.

"I hope you don't get into trouble for going inside," Linda said.

Gladys ignored this and wandered over to the back door. She narrowly missed Constable Tadmore striding over to the group she'd just left. Tadmore paused by Norm and gestured, pointing up at the automatic garage door.

Norm nodded and went with the constable.

Gladys walked by her bread racks stacked by the door. She decided to get them later after she'd seen to Albert and slipped inside the building.

There was no sign of Enid, the emergency responder, or the cop. Gladys didn't think there would be a problem with her being in the building. The accident scene was downstairs in the garage, not on her floor. She slid the key to Matthew's condo into the door lock.

"Excuse me, ma'am. Do you live in this building?"

Gladys swallowed and turned to look over her shoulder at the speaker. It was the tall dark-haired RCMP officer, the same one who had offered Enid a bottle of water earlier. The cop was standing four feet behind Gladys and watching her closely. She had her hands resting on her duty belt, and one hip cocked.

The creases of her light grey uniform shirt and dark trousers, sporting a reflective yellow stripe, were razor sharp. Every strand of her medium-brown hair was woven neatly into her French braid and the whole was pinned sleekly to the back of her head. Gladys could tell this was a no-nonsense type of person, but she wasn't trying to be intimidating, merely professional.

There was also curiosity in the cop's dark brown eyes, a keen intellect, and she was waiting for Gladys to answer her question.

"In the building, yes, but this is Matthew Wilkes' condo. He's away, so I'm letting his dog out to have a bio break. I hope that's okay?"

"I expect so."

Gladys nodded and turned the handle lever and whistled for the dog. "Come on, Albert, don't you have to go?"

There was the sharp clatter of nails on hardwood and Albert popped up at the door opening and kept going. From the pained expression on the dog's face, and his hurried exit, it was past time for him to be let outside. He bolted straight past both of women and made for the front entrance. Gladys bit her bottom lip, feeling guilty as she hurriedly grabbed the leash from inside the door and closed it, and then walked briskly after the dog.

"Don't let him go around back." The officer instructed. "I don't want him widdling on any evidence."

Gladys gave the cop a wave as she broke into a jog and opened the front door for the dog. Albert made it as far as the first lamp post in the smaller visitor's parking lot out front and lifted a leg.

"Sorry, buddy. I should have come in earlier." Gladys uncoiled the leash and leaned down to clip it onto his collar.

"You said you live in the building."

Gladys gave a little start as she straightened from attaching the lead. "Yes, I do." She turned back to the officer she hadn't heard approach.

"Sorry to startle you." The cop gave Gladys a half smile. "I'm Sergeant Lea Havelange. I'm leading this investigation."

"Gladys Wyatt, baker and resident of unit 102." She shook the officer's hand.

"You reported this incident, didn't you?" This really wasn't a question, but Gladys answered anyway.

"I did, yes." She blinked rapidly as the image of Dwayne lying under the garage door popped into her head again. She shivered and pushed it away, certainly not something she wanted to dwell on.

Gladys looked up at the officer. "I knew he was dead the moment I came around the corner. The way he was lying there..." She trailed off. Took a breath and continued. "I had to check, though, didn't I? I had to be sure there wasn't something I could do."

"What did you do? What did you touch?" A constable appeared at the sergeant's elbow. She even was taller than Havelange, thicker in build with jet-black hair and deeper dark eyes, looking almost black. "Preeceville, capture Mrs. Wyatt's statement in your notes please."

"Yes, ma'am." The constable had her occurrence note book out and a pen poised.

Gladys suddenly felt her throat tighten up. She cleared it and took a breath to calm down a notch. Rehashing the events was beginning to upset her and that wasn't helpful.

"It's all right," said the sergeant. "I know this can be hard to go through. Take your time."

Gladys nodded and clutched the leash tightly in her left hand. Albert sat down next to her and leaned on her calf. For some reason, the terrier's close proximity helped. "I reached under the door and took Dwayne's pulse. First on his wrist, and there was nothing." His skin had felt warm yet, but waxy. "I tried to move the door off him, I couldn't budge it. Enid tried to help me, too, after I yelled at her. That was probably a mistake, Edin became more hysterical. Anyway, to be sure Dwayne wasn't still alive. I reached under the door to touch the pulse in his neck." She swallowed. "There was none, he was so still."

Havelange nodded. "Thank you, it's good you told me this, I'll pass it on to the Ident team. I have something else I wanted to speak to you about."

"Oh? How can I help you?" Gladys quickly wiped the moisture from her eyes. Where had that come from? She didn't even like Dwayne.

At that moment, Albert chose to wander up to the cop. He went as close as the leash would allow and sniffed the sergeant's footwear.

"Behave, Albert." Gladys said absently, mostly to let Havelange know Albert was under her control. Which was important information for people who might not be familiar with dogs.

"He's fine." The cop leaned down and let Albert sniff her fist.

Apparently, she was acceptable, and the dog allowed her to scratch the top of his head. He gave her a puppy grin.

She straightened. "Can you tell me who could let us into Dwayne Davis' apartment? We haven't found his keys yet."

"Enid Lindquist, unit 101, she's the building manager."

"Ms. Lindquist is a bit overwrought at the moment."

"Oh, yes, well, I'm on the condo board, I know where the emergency keys are. I can let you in."

"That would great." She keyed the mic clipped to her tactical vest. "Pannu."

"Pannu, here."

"I've found a key holder who can let us in Dwayne Davis' apartment. Meet me in the hallway, please." She turned to Gladys and lifted an inquiring eyebrow.

"Oh." Gladys realized what the sergeant needed to know. "Dwayne's unit is on the ground floor, unit 103."

"On the ground floor." She relayed via her radio. Pannu responded in the affirmative.

"Here, Albert." Gladys called the dog back to her side. "You can go visit Blofeld while I get the keys." Albert fell into step with Gladys and they walked back to the building.

Havelange held the door for them. "Who's Blofeld?"

"He's my cat."

"Is he a white Persian?" She sounded amused.

"Of course."

Linda was in the hallway when they entered. "Do you need help with Enid?" She asked the sergeant.

"Possibly, that's very kind of you."

The younger woman shrugged. "She's my neighbour, so was Dwayne."

Two minutes later, Albert was left in Gladys' apartment, and she entered Enid's unit. Constable Pannu held the door open, and the sergeant followed her.

"All the duplicate keys are kept here." Gladys led the way to the utility room and paused at the manager's lock box which was attached to the wall inside the door and then extracted the spare key to Dwayne's unit.

The black metal case was unlocked. This was fortunate, she wouldn't have to disturb Enid, who sat at her kitchen table with her head down and arms wrapped around herself. She ignored the cup of tea Maude placed in front of her, but at least the woman was calmer.

Maude sipped her own cuppa as she leaned a hip on the counter edged. She raised her eyebrows in acknowledgement of Gladys and the cop. For her part, Gladys returned a weak smile and held up Dwayne's spare key and passed it to the sergeant.

"Enid?" Gladys approached the building manager. There was no response. "Enid, I've given the police Dwayne's spare key. They need to enter Dwayne's condo for their investigation." She glanced back at the sergeant, and she nodded.

Gladys patted Enid's shoulder and the other woman turned her head away. What could she say? It wasn't going to be all right.

They left Enid to Linda and Maude's care. "Is Enid going to be okay?" Gladys paused to ask Maude in a low tone. "It was a bit of a shock for her, I'm sure, but she seems almost catatonic."

"After a bad experience like this, I'm not surprised, but I think so." Maude put her cup down on the counter. "Come along, Enid." Maude persuaded the other woman to stand. Let's get you some place to lie down. I called your sister to come over from Mill Bay. She should be here in a bit. Linda's going to stay with you until she gets here." Maude put an arm around the larger woman and slowly walked Enid down the hallway to her bedroom.

Linda had been standing idle by the fridge. At the mention of her name, she blinked and looked around her. Abruptly she began to pick up dirty dishes and put them into the sink and generally made herself busy.

Maude returned and stopped by the sergeant. "Leslie and Steve should have the deceased loaded for Doctor Musoto by now. They'll want to be off on the next ferry. I should go."

"Thanks, talk to Constable Tadmore if there's anything further you need." They left the condo. Gladys gently shut the door behind her.

Maude gave the sergeant a nod and exited the building.

Sergeant Havelange walked over to the elevator and gestured at the out-of-order sign. "What's that about?"

"Oh, that happened a day or so ago. Linda had a water line connection break on the second floor in her unit. Some of the water leaked into the elevator shaft, so, Enid locked it down until the elevator can be inspected. Just in case." Gladys frowned as she thought of Lara. "But some people are still using the elevator anyway."

"How can they do that if the elevator is locked out?" Havelange asked.

"I don't know, but Lara Finkle seemed to manage it."

At the mention of the other woman's name, the sergeant's eyes narrowed slightly. "Yes, I remember Ms. Finkle." It didn't sound like the cop had a very high opinion of Gladys' neighbour.

The cop walked across the hallway to where Constable Pannu stood in front of Dwayne's door and handed her officer the key. "Open it up, please." She pulled on the same type of black latex gloves Pannu wore.

Awkwardly, Gladys waited to the right side of the door as it was unlocked. She wasn't sure if she should stay and answer any other questions or go back to her own place. Then the door was opened wide, and Gladys was rooted to the floor.

The sergeant also stood motionless in the opening for a moment as she sucked air in through her teeth. She was obviously gathering a first impression and it wasn't good.

Gladys had never been in Dwayne's apartment, now she was glad of it. Dwayne was obviously a hoarder.

Pannu stood at the sergeant's shoulder. "Wow, looks like a garage sale, or a pawn shop."

"Or a thief's stash." The sergeant placed her hands on her duty belt. "We might have a guess as to who was the cause of the local crime wave."

Gladys' jaw dropped as she realized the sergeant was right.

"We're gonna need some help with this." The constable shook his head.

"Exactly," the sergeant agreed and gestured to him. "We'll need Ident in here, now. Look over there by the television, or televisions, I should say."

Pannu tipped his head and narrowed his eyes. "Oh yeah, I get ya." He stepped back into the hallway and dug for his phone. With the constable busy on the phone, Gladys had a chance to see more easily into Dwayne's home.

Havelange stepped into the apartment doorway to look around, but didn't venture farther, probably because she couldn't. Items of all shapes and sizes were piled high and deep in the unit. The tiny foyer and the living room beyond were chock-a-block full. Golf clubs, lawn chairs, a sculpture of a pair of hands were haphazardly stacked on a patio table. Tools of all shapes and sizes were lined up against the east wall. Also, two table saws, a dozen drills and other hand power tools were piled on top. There were canvas tool bags filled to bursting with screwdrivers, hammers, utility knives, wrenches, and other smaller tools.

Gladys leaned forward and tipped her head to the right to see into the kitchen. His dining table was lined up with small appliances. Underneath the table, boxes with various electronics gear spilled out. Radar, navigation systems, and other electronics used for boats. Gladys blinked, it wasn't hard to imagine Dwayne as the village thief.

She stepped forward get a look at what had drawn Sergeant Havelange's attention by the widescreen TVs.

There, lined up in a wooden rack and propped against the wall was an assortment of firearms. Rifles, of various calibers and makes were leaned back in the rack. Underneath were black plastic boxes with molded handles. These look to be pistol cases.

Gladys' eyes widened. "Those weapons aren't stored properly. There's no trigger locks, everything is unsecured."

The sergeant turned around and gave Gladys an assessing frown. "Do you hold a possession and acquisition license, Mrs. Wyatt?

Gladys backed up into the hallway and tucked her hands into her pockets. She could feel her cheeks redden at being so forward, so snoopy. She shook her head. "No, my husband had a PAL. He was a hunter. While he was alive, we had a gun vault in the basement for his weapons and a separate lock box for his ammunition."

"Proper thing. What did you do with the weapons after his passing?"

"I made arrangements to transfer the titles to the rifles to my brother-in-law. He sold them for me."

The cop nodded. "So, none of these would be yours?"

"No, but if you find an electronic keyboard, it might belong to my granddaughter."

"I'll make a note of that."

Then a thought occurred to Gladys, and she looked at Dwayne's key ring hanging from the door lock. "Sergeant Havelange, you might want to come down to the basement with me. I can show you where Dwayne's storage locker is. I have a feeling we'll find more stolen property there. That second key on the ring will open it."

"Once I've supervised the removal of the firearms, that would be very helpful, Mrs. Wyatt, thank you."

The next half hour was busy as members of the forensic unit swarmed Dwayne's condo and removed the weaponry. They also found several long-bladed knives. All the items were efficiently tagged, bagged, and carted away for further examination.

Once this was done, the sergeant turned back to Gladys who had waited patiently across the hall. "If you'll show me the storage locker?"

Mostly Gladys had been curious as to what else the authorities would find. "Of course," she agreed. At that moment the setting sun streamed into the kitchen window and glanced off a collection of shiny items stack together on a silver tray seated on the counter. "That's Enid's sterling silver tea service," Gladys blurted, not realizing she'd said the words out loud until the sergeant spoke.

"Are you sure?" The sergeant's eyes narrowed as she focused on the pile of silver.

"As sure as I can be at this distance. We had tea at her place during the condo board meeting only yesterday. There can't be two like it in the village."

"Pannu, make sure that's followed up on." She jerked her thumb over her shoulder. "Check to see if Ms. Lindquist's service is missing. Ask Tadmore to join to us in the garage."

"Will do." Pannu said as he made a note in his occurrence notepad.

Havelange nodded and pulled the keys out of the lock. "Let's go," she said to Gladys.

Chapter Nineteen

It had been made clear by the contents of Dwayne Davis' apartment that he had definitely been the village thief. Even though he'd been the one who stole her family's things, Gladys was surprised she didn't harbour more anger toward the man. Maybe because he was no longer among them. The dead should be forgiven for their sins otherwise they haunted the living.

As Gladys led the sergeant to the condo building's lower level, she realized Dwayne would have known when she wasn't home. Her days were full of routine. Bake most mornings, and then make deliveries in the afternoons. Except for the cafe, that delivery was done as soon as the loaves were cool enough to bag.

Somehow Dwayne had gained entrance to her condo. Did he pick her lock? This realization made her queasy to think Dwayne had pawed through all of her belongings. Dwayne had stolen Micky's wedding ring.

"He forgot to lock my patio door," she said, and her steps slowed as she realized she'd said this out load.

"When did you discover this? After you were robbed?"

"Yes." Gladys looked at the sergeant.

The cop held up the keys in her hand. "I'm fairly sure I know how Davis got into your condo."

"He took the keys from Enid but left he patio door was let open."

"Someone might have been in the hallway. He could have left by the other door. We will have to confirm my suspicions, so don't mention anything to your neighbours until I do." Havelange lowered her hand.

Gladys nodded and they continued down the concrete steps.

When Gladys thought about it, she had a feeling she knew why Dwayne had turned to thievery. His reasons were probably the same as her own were. They both needed money to afford to live in this crazy condo building.

Even so, stealing from your friends and neighbours to make ends meet was not the way to go. He should have sold his unit if he couldn't afford it. Maybe she should do the same, but where would she go?

Gladys pushed these thoughts away as she led the cop down the steps. They arrived at the parking level. It was at least ten degrees cooler here in the huge open area below the building. The underground parking was divided up with white lines separating the spaces.

The sergeant paused and gestured toward the north end of the garage. "Who owns that car?" The cop gestured to the far corner where a vehicle was parked under a dust cover. "My neighbour, Matthew Wilkes." Freddie told Gladys some time ago Matthew's prize possession was an Aston Martin, but she didn't actually know firsthand, nor did she particularly care.

"The space on the left is Matthew's as well. It's empty, his daily driver is no doubt parked at the airport."

"Albert's owner?"

"Yes, he should be back home Sunday if you need to speak to him."

The cop nodded. "We will be doing vehicle checks. And the next one?"

"Freddie Freeman's jeep." Rusty, dented, and mud spattered, the vehicle fit her second-floor neighbour to a T. Gladys frowned. "I wonder how Freddie can afford to park down here."

"I wonder how Mr. Freeman can afford a condo in this building at all." The cop countered. "But we will find out. And the next car, who owns it?"

"Enid does." The electric-blue Nissan sedan was meticulously clean and shiny. "The empty spot next to Enid is Lara Finkle's."

"There are slots available for several more vehicles."

"Yes, but as I said, it's pricy to park down here. Dwayne's parking spot is at the farthest end closest to the storage lockers." His car was not parked there now. It was located just below the ramp.

Gladys looked right, as they got moving again. They passed the spot in front of the garage door where the accident had happened. She was relieved to see Dwayne's body had been taken away. Still, the empty spot under the door made her swallow to relieve her dry throat.

Yellow and black police tape sectioned off the area. There was a large wet mark on the exit ramp. Right about where she'd found his body. Gladys shifted her gaze. She didn't know if the wet mark was from Dwayne's blood or from the cleanup. Best not to dwell on it in any case.

She noted the twenty-foot square automatic sliding door was retracted half-way onto its track across the ceiling, leaving the entrance/exit wide open now. The door didn't appear to be broken or bent. Nor did the door need to be held up by artificial means, like a rope, to safely suspend it over the opening. Norm must have helped open it. He'd have the mechanical knowhow.

Gladys looked away from the scene to the familiar gold convertible parked six feet or so below the ramp. The driver's side door was open. "Dwayne was carrying a box of items with him when I saw him at the marina Wednesday during the farmers' market. That box might be in the trunk of his car."

"You think the box contains more stolen items?" The cop gave Gladys a sidelong look.

"I think so, yes."

"Interesting." The sergeant nodded.

On the other side of the caution tape, forensic people were kitted up in white disposable coveralls, gloves, and shoe coverings. Dwayne's car was being examined as was the surrounding area.

"Dwayne must have been going out when he was...when the..." Her words trailed off.

"When he was killed?" The sergeant was watching Gladys closely again.

She came to an abrupt halt. "Yes. I should mention I saw Dwayne getting booted out of the marina bar Wednesday."

The cop stopped and Gladys did as well. "Oh? And why was that?"

"Big Chris, the bartender, was angry Dwayne was trying to sell things to the bar's customers. He told Dwayne not to try it again or he'd ban him from the premises."

"I see. You think he was trying to sell some of the stolen goods there?"

"I think so, but I don't actually know. I just saw him put the box back in his trunk."

"Thank you for telling me."

Gladys nodded and turned away to continue to the storage area. Then her head came up. "Wait a minute." A frown spread across Gladys' features as she came to a halt again and looked up at the sergeant. "Don't all garage doors have sensors setup to stop the door from closing if its path were obstructed? That door should stop at least a foot from the ground. How could Dwayne have been killed like that?"

"Good question." Sergeant looked back at Gladys steadily.

Gladys stared at the cop and her frown melted into a wide-eyed stare as the obvious occurred to her. She had to ask. "Was Dwayne murdered?"

"As you said, there are several safeguards to prevent automatic doors from closing on an obstacle. Garage doors don't fall down by themselves." The sergeant paused. "That is, unless the door was tampered with." She raised a single dark eyebrow at Gladys.

The older woman slowly shook her head. "My lord."

"Yes," agreed Havelange. "How well did you get on with Mr. Davis?"

The question sounded innocent, but Gladys was not fooled. Did the senior officer consider her a suspect? That was simply crazy. "Dwayne wasn't my favourite person by any means, but we didn't interact much. He kept to his patch, and I kept to mine."

"Was Mr. Davis a customer of your bakery business?"

Gladys shook her head. "No, but he voted on my side to allow cottage businesses to operate from our homes. The vote is in the board meeting minutes."

"I'd like a copy of the minutes."

"I can get them for you, no problem. You should also know Enid and Dwayne had a disagreement about unpaid parking fees and she took away his key fob that automatically opens the garage door." Gladys turned to look at the door as she thought about Enid.

Officer Tadmore came down the stairs and jogged over to join them.

Gladys glanced his way but continued with her thought. "That's why Dwayne had to get out of his car to open the door manually." Was he set up?

The sergeant turned to Tadmore. "Make a note to ask Ms. Lindquist about the disagreement over unpaid parking fees and Mr. Davis' garage door opener."

"Will do. Should I go speak to her now?"

"Not just yet." Havelange turned back to Gladys. "When was that confrontation?"

"Yesterday, at the evening condo meeting. Linda and Freddie were there too."

"The cop nodded. "Thank you, is there anything else you think we should know?" Tadmore had his occurrence note pad out and was taking notes.

Gladys rolled her lip over her bottom teeth as she considered the question. "Linda said she lost three hundred dollars in bingo winnings from her cookie jar."

Tadmore wrote that down too.

His boss frowned at her constable. "That theft wasn't reported?"

"I don't believe so, Sergeant."

Both RCMP officers looked down at Gladys expectantly.

Gladys shrugged one shoulder. "I don't honestly know."

"Anything else come to mind?" Tadmore asked.

Ah well, in for a penny and all that. "You already know about Freddie Freeman's pot operation?" It was not actually a question.

Tadmore snorted. "That's a fact. He's pretty proud of it too."

The cop in charge raised one dark eyebrow in question at the constable and made a noise in her throat.

He glanced sideways at his boss and composed his expression, going bland.

"Please continue, Mrs. Wyatt," Havelange said as she turned back to Gladys.

"Right, well, apparently Dwayne demanded a cut of the profits from Freddie, or he'd turn Freddie in to you. The thing is, Freddie gives the weed away, or so he says. I don't know, I'm not one of his customers. I'm not a fan of pot, smoking is smoking."

"Mr. Freeman did tell us he gives the weed away to the 'needy,'" Tadmore offered with a small disbelieving smile. "However, he didn't say anything about being blackmailed."

"Still, we'll need another conversation with Mr. Freeman regardless." The sergeant said. "Do you know if any of the other residents are Mr. Freeman's customers?"

"I'm afraid I couldn't tell you." Gladys shook her head.

"Ma'am." One of the forensic people called over to them to get the Sergeant's attention. "You might want to see this."

"Excuse me a moment, please." She narrowed her eyes slightly at Tadmore before she strode off to the car.

Gladys spotted the 'keep an eye on her' look and the constable's nod. He merely gave Gladys a friendly smile when her gaze fell again on the young man.

Before they allowed the sergeant to look at what they'd found she had to put on shoe coverings and gloves.

Gladys watched the activity. "Have you found my husband's wedding ring?"

"Sorry, not as far as I know, not yet anyway. With the amount of stolen goods to go through it may take a while." He left the unsaid whether Davis still had her things, but the statement hung in the air between them, nonetheless.

Sadly, she nodded and shifted her stance to look back at the gold vehicle.

Two others, dressed in white coveralls, were with the sergeant as they clustered around the trunk. The shorter figure in the shapeless garment was still obviously female. She pointed to areas inside of the truck lid. Then she mimed an abrupt downward strike and fanned her gloved hands out and pointed to the areas again.

The sergeant nodded and they both stepped back to talk. Gladys frowned. She still could not hear what was said.

The second, taller figure, probably male by the width of his shoulders, stepped forward. He took photographs from every possible angle. He then exchanged his camera for evidence bags as his co-worker stepped forward again.

A set of keys was removed and bagged. The cardboard box Gladys had mentioned was lifted out, taken away, and deposited on a folding table to be examined. Then a garbage bag wrapped item was removed. It was approximately three feet long and rectangular. The male peeled away some of the black trash bag.

Gladys pointed at the instrument. "Hey, that's my Maisy's keyboard."

Tadmore placed a restraining hand on her arm. "And your granddaughter will get it back once we no longer need it as evidence."

"Maisy was practicing the keyboard two nights ago." Anger rolled over Gladys. She balled her hands into fists. "He probably heard her. How, how dare he." She sputtered a few more choice words she would be embarrassed about later.

"Please, Mrs. Wyatt, please calm down. He can't hurt your granddaughter now nor take anything else. Mr. Davis wasn't the violent type, merely a thief."

She rounded him. "Not the violent type? He threw Albert off the balcony."

Tadmore blinked and dropped his hand to frown at her. "When was this?"

"Almost six weeks ago. Albert is too fat to get under the balcony railings. We think the thief broke into Matthew's apartment and when Albert made a fuss, Dwayne tried to shut him up."

The cop wrote this down. "Was anything stolen?"

Gladys nodded her head. "There wasn't much to take. Matthew is a minimalist. He has four prize possessions. Albert, his car, his computer, and a cappuccino maker as far as I know. The only thing missing is the cappuccino maker."

"Any ideas on how Davis got into the apartment?"

"That's your job to figure out." Gladys felt ashamed the minute the words flew out and she covered her mouth with her right hand. "I'm sorry." She dropped her hand. "I should never have said anything like that. I'm just worked up about Maisy. That creepy son of a–" She made her words stop and clamped her mouth shut. She swallowed and got a grip on herself. "Your sergeant seems to think she knows how Dwayne did it, but she asked me not to say anything."

The Constable gave her a conceding nod. "I understand. With everything in his apartment and probably what we find in his storage unit, it will take time to photograph the stolen goods, catalogue them, and finally release them back to their owners. Maisy will get her keyboard back, I promise." Tadmore sounded sincere. "The more quickly things are reported the more quickly the items may be returned."

Another thought had just occurred to Gladys. "Then there is the fact Dwayne is dead and there's no one to prosecute for all the robberies."

"That could be true." Tadmore stepped back as his boss returned.

What did that mean?

The sergeant gestured for Gladys to lead the way. "Well, Mrs. Wyatt, shall we proceed?"

"Yes, of course. The locker facilities are over here." She turned on her heel and led the way to the line of grey metal doors along the back wall. Thankfully, well away from the ramp and the garage door. Each had a slot for a name tag, except Dwayne Davis'. His read 'President' and was attached to the third grey metal door.

Havelange handed Tadmore the keys and he leaned down to open the padlock.

Gladys stood back out of the way. Now that she'd seen proof of Dwayne's crimes against her friends and family with her own eyes, she felt much less empathy.

Still, she was curious to find out what he had squirreled away inside the storage unit. Somewhere, either here or in Dwayne's condo, she hoped they would find Micky's wedding band and coin collection. She so hoped Dwayne had not found time to fence the items. The coins would be a loss but did not mean as much to her as Micky's ring did.

Deftly, Tadmore removed the lock and rolled up the door. A cloud of dust swirled about and rose up. It was dark inside the unit. Both cops snapped on flashlights. This room too, was a jumble of items.

"There should be a light on the right-hand wall," Gladys pointed out helpfully.

"Thank you." Tadmore found the metal switch box on the cinderblock wall.

Glaring white light illuminated the interior of the storage area. This space was better organized than Dwayne's apartment. The contents looked like any storage unit belonging to any apartment dweller. Well, except for the large metal box in the middle of the concrete floor. It was an old fashioned black safe, covered in a brownish-grey patina. The dark gold lettering on the front on the front read, 'International Safe Co. Limited' there was a combination wheel and lever handle. Below that, 'Fort Erie, Ontario.' The safe looked solid and very heavy. It rested on a dolly or hand truck as Micky used to call such things which would make moving the heavy metal cube easier.

"Obviously the safe didn't belong to Davis." Tadmore gestured to the scattering of tools spread out on the floor, in front of the steel box.

There were dents and chips out of the safe's paint around the handle. It looked as though Dwayne had been trying to crack the safe and had no idea how to go about it.

"I'm betting this is the safe Lara Finkle reported missing." Tadmore squatted down to get a better look at the markings.

So that was what Lara had been upset about earlier in the week. Gladys lifted her eyebrows, maybe Arlie was right after all. Maybe Lara still had some of the embezzled money from her deceased boyfriend.

"Thank you, Mrs. Wyatt, we'll take it from here."

Gladys glanced over at the sergeant. "No problem, let me know if you need anything else." Since she was dismissed, Gladys escaped.

"Close it up Tadmore, we need Ident to do their thing before we paw through the contents. We'll make sure the apartment is locked up as well. There's plenty here and in the apartment to start with. We need more resources to handle the rest of the evidence cataloguing."

"Meal break, and then get back to it?" Tadmore rolled the door back down.

"Yep, Jane's got the soup on."

Gladys was happy to be out of it. She trotted up the steps and went to the back door to get her abandoned bread racks.

Chapter Twenty

G ladys returned to the foyer and was in time to see Linda abruptly push the stairwell door open. Her second-floor neighbour stalked across the hallway to apartment 103 carrying a yellow crowbar. She looked strange in her tangerine flower print dress and matching sandals lugging the tool.

"Linda," Gladys said cautiously. "What are you doing?" She put the bread racks down by her door.

The RCMP had locked up. They'd left a constable by the garage door entrance but had not posted a guard on Dwayne's unit.

"Enid's sister arrived and told me rather rudely I wasn't needed. So, I left her to it." Linda hefted the crowbar in a meaningful way. "Now, I'm taking the rest of my stuff back."

"You can't do that."

Linda grabbed the yellow and black caution tape with her left hand and ripped it down. "Oh, I'm betting I can." The tape stuck to her hand. She tried to wave it off unsuccessfully.

"The RCMP have designated Dwayne's condo a crime scene."

"I don't care." Linda peeled the tape off and awkwardly balled it up to discard onto the floor. "I'm done waiting for others to help me."

"The police haven't even begun processing all of stolen goods in there yet. Well, except for the firearms. You'll get into trouble for fiddling with a crime scene, please don't do this."

"I want my stuff. Dwayne is dead, it's not like he'll go to jail for stealing from me, the big creep." She tried the door, of course it was locked. "Figures, that's why I brought my own key." Linda grasped the crowbar tightly and stabbed the straight end between the doorjamb and lock.

Gladys walked forward cautiously, her hands raised in a placating gesture. Her friend was upset. From the moment Gladys had met Linda, she knew the younger woman was wound a bit tight. The day's events would have made it worse, and she needed careful handling. "I've seen inside, there are too many stolen items to find anything easily."

Linda turned and locked her gaze on Gladys. "You've been in Dwayne's condo? When?"

"This afternoon, not fifteen minutes ago. We stopped in to get the keys from the lock box in Enid's utility room. You were the apartment cleaning up."

The younger woman looked down at her feet, blinking. "Oh yeah, I remember."

Eyebrows raised at this lapse, Gladys decided to continue carefully. "There's simply too much stuff, the place is chock-a-block full. It's all evidence right now as far as the police are concerned." She thought she might be able to take the crowbar away, so Gladys edge closer. "We have to wait. I'm certain there are police procedures for this type of thing, and a process on how we get our stuff back." She reached out her left hand slowly to take the pry bar from the other woman

"They'll be too slow. We'll probably have to wait a year to get our stuff back."

"The cops are coming back here shortly. One or two are probably just outside. You could ask the sergeant when she gets back if you can have your things, but can't you wait a bit?" Her hand was mere inches from the tool.

"I'm done waiting." Linda batted Gladys' hand away. "I want my things back." Linda frowned as she looked at first one end of the crowbar then the other, like she was trying to figure out how to use the tool.

"Where did you get that crowbar anyway?"

"I found it."

Sure, she did. Gladys had an extremely unsettling feeling about the situation. She had to try again. "But the police haven't given anyone permission to go into Dwayne's apartment yet. Please don't do anything foolish."

"I'm done letting other people boss me around." The younger woman hefted the crowbar again and jammed the teeth or claws between the doorframe and the door once more. The tool bit deeper into the wooden doorframe this time. Linda leaned on it and cracked the wood on the doorjamb.

Gladys' words were falling on deaf ears. She knew Linda was not going to be dissuaded by her arguments.

Watching the frame splinter, she realized Linda was stronger than Gladys would ever have expected. "You really need to stop. You have to be breaking several kinds of laws." She tried again anyway.

"What are they going to do? Arrest me for taking back my own stuff?"

Gladys' caution was rapidly evolving into fear. This wasn't a side of her friend she'd ever seen before. It was disturbing.

"I thought you said you were missing some money? I doubt you'll find it just lying around in there." She tried logic this time. "How are you going to identify what money is yours, even if Dwayne hasn't already spent it?"

She needed to do something. Who should she call? Medical help because Linda was having a meltdown or the RCMP? If she merely walked outside, she could grab the attention of the constable left to mind the entrance to the parking garage. She could let them know what was going on. Gladys wondered when she had turned into such a ditherer.

"He took more than money from me." Linda leaned on the pry bar and the doorjamb wood screamed as it split further. "So much more."

The noise startled Gladys. She edged away from Linda and toward the back door. However, Linda's words stopped her. "What?"

"Dwayne took my mother's antique, twenty-four-karat gold pendant, and her matching earrings. That's all I have from her. I never knew my mom. She died when I was still a baby. He also took my father's gold pocket watch." Linda turned and looked at Gladys. Her eyes were fever bright. "It was just the two of us. I used to tag along on Dad's jobs when I was a kid. I'd help him with the installations. I became quite good at it, but Dad didn't want to see me installing garage doors for a living. He wanted more for me. So, I went to university instead and got my teaching degree. In my last year at university, Dad hired a guy to help him because I wasn't there. Forth day on the job, the new guy didn't secure the door or engage the sensors properly, and three panels fell on my dad. Killed him instantly." She turned away, lifting the crowbar again and roughly jammed it deeper between the door and the jamb. Her knuckles were white with the strength of her grip and her hands trembled. From intensity or trepidation, Gladys did not know.

Instead, Gladys focused on her words. Linda's father had been a garage door installer, and she had worked with him. It was possible Linda knew how to disengage the door sensors and drop the door on a person, but would she? Gladys swallowed, but it didn't help. Her throat, like her mouth, was completely dry. She dug for her cell phone in her back pocket.

The younger woman twisted the tool and the wood screamed again. "Dwayne took everything of value from my jewelry case. He probably planned to pawn it all."

There was no point in questioning if Dwayne was the thief. "Did you catch him in the act?"

Linda shook her head. "I figured it was him. He left his muddy boot prints on my carpets. Those pointy-toed cowboy boots are easy to identify. It was like he didn't care if I thought it was him. But I knew for sure at the condo meeting." Linda turned back to look at Gladys. "He took out a gold watch, a pocket watch, exactly like my dad used to have. I had it placed next to my mom's jewelry. He made sure I saw it when he checked the time. I knew that was Dad's watch as soon as Dwayne opened it." Her eyes burned. "That's the first thing I took back." She paused with trying to break into the condo and slipped her left hand into her front jean pocket. Slowly, Linda drew out the gold pocket watch she had spoken of and pressed the button to pop the case the open.

Gladys stared wide-eyed at the time piece. If this was the watch Dwayne had on him, how had Linda gotten it? The answer was self-evident. A cold knot took up residence in Gladys' stomach.

"There used to be a photo of my mom inside. Dwayne must have taken it out."

"How...uh, how do you know that's your father's watch?" Gladys asked as gently as she could.

Linda let go of the crowbar and it stayed stuck in place between the door and the frame. She closed the case and turned it over. "To my darling Chester, happy birthday, love Amanda." She read off the back of the watch and raised sad eyes to Gladys. "Chester and Amanda Leechie were my parents."

"I'm so sorry." Gladys could not think of anything else to say.

Linda nodded and put the watch away and then turned back to her work. The door's frame splintered as Linda put her weight against the lever. It broke into pieces. "Dwayne knew I had money stashed away too. I think he heard me telling Freddie about the pearl-pink moped I planned to buy a couple of weeks ago." Wooden shards and paint pelted the hallway carpet, littering the floor. "Dwayne came to Freddie's place just as I was leaving. I think that's when he threatened Freddie too." The hallway door slowly swung open. "Dwayne was a thief and a bully. He got what he deserved." Linda dropped the crowbar. It hit the doormat with a muffled thud as she entered the apartment. "I only want back what's mine."

Gladys took another step backward. Her eye was caught by a red-brown stain on the outer curve of the neck of the yellow crowbar. Was that blood? She stared at the long thick metal bar and knew with a chilling certainty the stain had to be Dwayne's blood. The image of the forensic people showing the Sergeant Dwayne's truck flashed in her mind's eye.

She clutched her phone in one hand. She didn't know what to do. Linda was cool, detached, and yet livid. A deep burning cold anger was driving her. She turned to get to the back door and took two steps.

"Gladys." Linda had returned to the opening she'd made. She stared steadily at the older woman as she leaned down and picked up the crowbar again. "Dwayne took your things too, things that meant the world to you." She crossed to where Gladys stood. "I'm sure all our things are here somewhere." Linda grasped Gladys' arm in a tight grip. "Let's look, shall we?" Linda's stare met Gladys' and she propelled the older woman to the open doorway. "We'll start here." Then she let go of Gladys to slap the tool across the palm of her left hand. Linda was only a foot away, well within the range of the crowbar if she swung it at her.

"I'll be right behind you." Gladys nodded and swallowed hard on her rising terror.

"Good." Linda walked forward and began to pick her way through the hoard. "Look, isn't that Enid's tea service?" She used the pry bar to point into the kitchen.

Hastily Gladys turned around and ran to her own apartment. Quickly she opened and slammed the door behind. Flipped on the deadbolt, and then the doorknob lock for good measure. Her heart was pounded crazily in her chest as she retreated to the kitchen. She punched in 911 on her phone and listened to it ring.

Albert got up from his basket and stretched. He ignored Gladys to check the cat dishes instead.

Too agitated to be still, Gladys began to pace the length of her kitchen. Two circuits around the room and then emergency dispatcher came on the line.

"911 what is the nature of your emergency?" said a flat female voice.

Gladys didn't know how to describe what was going on, so she simply said, "I need the police."

"May I have your name please?" Gladys gave it. "Yes, ma'am what's happening?"

The dog, having finished off Blofeld's dry food, sat down to watched Gladys march back and forth from living room to kitchen with one brown ear cocked.

"I want Sergeant Havelange, I think she's still investigating here somewhere. She's lead on the Dwayne Davis murder. I'm afraid someone else might get hurt."

"I need your address, please." The voice said more urgently.

Gladys gave it.

There was hammering on her door. Albert barked sharply and Gladys dropped her phone. The device clattered to the floor.

"Gladys, I found my golf clubs" Linda asked through the door. "Don't you want your stuff?"

"I...I'll wait for the police to release it to me," she called back to Linda. "I'm in no hurry." She snatched up the mobile phone. "She's at my door, I have to go." Gladys whispered sharply into the phone.

"Wait, don't–"

Gladys didn't want to, but she ended the call. She didn't want Linda to figure out she'd called the cops. If she could break into Dwayne's apartment, she could do the same to Gladys' before the police arrived. Who knew what else Linda was capable of?

"You were right, there's a ton of stuff in there." Linda called through the door. "Can you give me a hand? I can't seem to find my mother's jewelry."

Silently, Gladys shook her head. There was no way in hell she was going out there.

"Can I help you, Linda?" It was Maisy's voice.

Gladys' eyes opened wide in horror. "Oh, dear Lord, no." Her granddaughter was back from work. She ran to the door and flipped off the locks to open it.

Albert dashed out past her feet to greet his favourite person in the world next to Matthew Wilkes.

"Hi, little buddy," Maisy leaned down to scratch the dog's ears.

Gladys was happy to see the pry bar was back lying by the other unit's door where Linda must have dropped it again. Next to it was a set of Taylor golf clubs leaning against the wall. "Hello, Sweetie." Gladys' greeting was bright and forced. "You had a call on my phone while you were at work. The number's in my recent calls. You take Albert for his walk, I'll help Linda." Gladys stepped out into the hallway and handed Maisy her phone.

"Okay," Maisy said and gave her grandmother an odd look. "I'll call them later. I should take Albert for a walk first." Maisy grinned at the wee dog as he jumped around. "Walk is your trigger word, isn't it?"

Gladys leaned back into the condo and snatched the leash from the hook by the door. "Good plan." She closed her door and walked past Linda to hand Maisy the leash with a trembling hand. She'd do anything to get her granddaughter out of harm's way.

"Thanks, Grandma." Maisy quickly clipped the leash on Albert's collar and escorted him out the front door.

"Well, Linda." Gladys swallowed. She gestured to the open door across the hall. "Let go find your stolen things, shall we?"

Linda gave the older woman a beaming smile.

Gladys breathed out slowly as she followed the younger woman into Dwayne's apartment. While Linda almost sounded more like her old self, Gladys knew she had to be careful not to 'trigger' her. She just hoped the RCMP would return and find them in time before anything else fatal happened. She was certain her 911 call would speed things along.

"What are you two doing?"

Gladys looked across the hall to see Enid glowered at them from her open doorway.

"We are getting our stuff back," Linda said tersely.

"Enid, dear, you should be lying down. Let them be." A tiny bird-like woman with silver hair in a red top and jeans was behind the building manager. She must be Enid's sister.

"I'm fine, Winnie, don't fuss." Enid strode forward.

Gladys willed the bigger woman to see the crowbar. Maybe Enid would figure it out and call the police.

Linda used her left foot to push the tool out of Enid's path and against the wall. "I wouldn't want you to trip," she said sweetly to the building manager.

Enid ignored both Gladys and Linda as she marched past them and into Dwayne's apartment. She stalked down the narrow path through the stolen goods, straight to the kitchen counter where her silver tea service was chaotically stacked on its tray. "I'm taking back my things too." She snatched up the set and marched out, again, past Linda and Gladys. "The dirty little snake," she muttered, then slammed her door shut.

"Huh," said Linda. "She's never been much help."

With a hesitant nod, Gladys had to concede Linda did have a point.

As Gladys looked on, Linda poked and prodded boxes and bags. Gladys avoided touching anything. Desperately she was beginning to hope she might have been mistaken. Was Linda even capable of smacking someone on the head with a crowbar? What about the garage door? How did that figure in? Then Linda began pushing piles of items over and throwing things about. "There's nothing here!" Linda sounded frustrated and angry. "I don't see any jewelry."

Gladys bit her lip. Should she tell Linda about the safe in the storage unit? Did Sergeant Havelange leave a constable to guard the storage unit?

The 911 operator should have contacted the officers by now. Or maybe, she'd called back on Gladys' mobile to talk to Maisy. "There's lots of places he could have put small things like jewelry. What about his bedroom?"

"Aha!" Linda dashed off down the hallway. "Oh, my Lord, it's filthy in here." Linda returned quickly. She shoved over a pile of lawn furniture, and it crashed to the floor making Gladys jump.

Linda's frustration was growing again, and she picked up a hammer out of a toolbox and advanced on the widescreen TVs. Gladys knew it was important to keep Linda calm, and swinging a hammer, damaging other people's property wasn't the answer.

Her decision was made. "What about Dwayne's storage locker?"

The younger woman came to a halt and turned to look at Gladys.

"What if Dwayne hid more stuff down there? It's worth a look, don't you think?"

Linda dropped the hammer and Gladys breathed again.

"Yes, it is. Come on." Linda marched out but paused in the hallway to snatch up her crowbar. She gave Gladys a chilling smile. "I might need my universal key." Her step was determined as she exited Dwayne's apartment, crossed the hall, and swung open the stairway door to descend to the basement. Linda waved at her. "Let's go."

Gladys thought about creating a delay. Find some excuse not to follow Linda, but what if Maisy came back too soon before the police arrived?

Resolutely, Gladys walked over to the stairwell.

Linda followed her neighbour down the stairs.

Chapter Twenty-One

Gladys slowed her steps as much as she could, but still she reached the basement parking area much too quickly. The area was deserted. Dwayne's car was gone and so too, were the police. The large garage door was now closed with an out-of-order sign, and police caution tape across the area. The garage was colder now and smelled of damp and antiseptic, the kind that seemed to penetrate right to the back of the throat.

Linda brushed past Gladys and was already halfway across the open area, marching ahead.

Her steps echoed hollowly as Gladys crossed the open stretch of concrete floor to the storage units. The urge to run back up the stairs was almost overwhelming. Why she plodded over to storage unit number three she would never be able to explain.

She found Linda trying to perform the same trick she'd executed on Dwayne's apartment door. The difference was the locker unit's door was metal and designed with anti-theft in mind. This metal door was latched on the bottom, and more robust. Linda was having a difficult time trying to wedge the crowbar under the edge.

Impatiently, Linda batted the torn and tattered yellow caution tape out of her way. The younger woman growled as she tried again to jam the end of the pry bar under a new section of door which hadn't yet been dented as a result of her previous attempts.

Sweat dampened Linda's hairline. Thin blonde hair escaped from her ponytail and stuck to her face as she once more leaned on the pry bar. Abruptly the crowbar popped loose, and Linda stumbled back, close to losing her balance.

Staying well back, Gladys was not going to suggest anything which would help Linda break into the unit.

Baring her teeth at the stubborn door, Linda regained her feet and stood back.

Gladys was becoming more alarmed as each moment passed. Her neighbour appeared to be losing her grip even more on her temper.

Linda swung the bar and gave the roller door a sharp whack. The lock attached to the door hasp jumped and emitted a clunk as it hit the concrete floor.

With a menacing glare Linda stared down at the offender. "Aha!" She ran forward and wedged the lever behind the hasp that was fastened through a loop of metal by the pad lock. One good pull and the screws screeched as they were forcefully pried out of the frame. Linda repeated the maneuver and the screws let go of the hasp all together.

As the small fasteners rained down on the concrete floor, Gladys became more anxious. What would she do when Linda couldn't get the safe opened?

The crowbar hit the floor with a clang and a clatter as Linda grabbed the tab strap attached to the handle. She heaved upward and the door easily rolled open to reveal the dark interior.

Gladys didn't have to tell Linda about the light switch. Linda had her own storage unit three doors down. Light flooded the unit, and the same items were revealed.

"A safe, no wonder there was nothing of real value in Dwayne's apartment." Linda advanced on the steel box and tried the handle. Of course, it was locked.

Gladys said nothing, not correcting Linda's assumption the safe belonged Dwayne.

Gladys took a couple steps backward. What would the police make of the fact Linda's fingerprints were now on the safe along with Dwayne's?

Linda walked around the metal box as it squatted on the dolly.

"You're implicating yourself in the robberies by touching the evidence. Linda, you need to stop."

Her neighbour ignored Gladys' words and walked around the safe again examining it. "How do I get inside without the combination?" They were diverted by the sound of the stairway door opening again.

Gladys snapped her head around, hoping to see a one of the constables, but it was merely Lara Finkle. The woman, dress in a lime-green sundress and matching high heeled sandals paused as she looked over at Gladys and Linda.

She strode in their direction. "There's a cop blocking the garage door, and someone's broken into Dwayne's condo. I doubt the police would leave the door open. Enid doesn't care–" Her words cut off as she changed her tone. "Hey!" Lara yelled at them; her walk changed to a trotting run. She advanced on the open storage locker. "What do you think you're doing?"

Gladys watched mutely as the blonde woman ran past her. The heels of Lara's green sandals against the concrete echoed loudly as she hurried to the open storage locker. "This is Dwayne's locker."

"Duh." Linda looked back at Lara. "If it's any of your business, we are getting our valuables back. Dwayne was a thief."

Linda said and leaned over the safe. She tried to wedge the crowbar between the safe door and the frame.

"Get away from there!" Lara snarled and hip-checked Linda aside making the younger woman stumbled back in surprise. She dropped the tool and it clanged to the floor of storage unit.

Then things got weirder as Lara dropped to her bare knees in front of the safe and wrapped her arms around the metal box in a hug. "Where have you been?" She spoke to the object like it was a well-loved lost child.

Linda's look of shock turned appalled. "What do you think you're doing?" For a moment Gladys feared Linda would lose her temper and hurt the older woman.

"This is my safe." The heated intensity in Lara's tone made Linda blink. "Dwayne must have stolen it. If he wasn't dead already, I would have killed him."

Linda moved a step forward. "Can you open it?"

Lara ignored Linda as she ran her hands over the safe like she was looking for damage. Apparently satisfied, she sat back on her heels.

Eagerly, Linda bent to retrieve her pry bar and moved up beside Lara.

"Please, please, please." Lara whispered as her fingertips brushed the central dial. She turned the disk to the left and stopped at the number 9.

They heard a faint click and Lara turned the lever handle to swing the thick metal door open. She rifled around inside, pulled out brown envelops, a stack of certificates bound with an elastic band, and a small velvet-covered box. There were other items, but it was these things Lara appeared to urgently want.

She leaned back and noticed Linda staring at her. "What are you doing with that crowbar? Were you going to try and open my safe with that? This is mine. You have no right."

"Oh really?" Linda's tone was snaky. "Dwayne stole from me too. I want to see if my mother's jewelry is in that safe."

Abruptly, Lara used her left hand to slam the safe door shut and then she spun the dial, re-locking the safe. "You're not getting in there." She rose unsteadily to her feet and walked away. "I'm just glad that crazy idiot didn't know I kept the safe on the hitch, otherwise he'd have stolen every–"

The stairwell door swung open again and Constable Tadmore briskly strode across the open parking area. He came to a stop few feet away from them. "Freeze right there, all of you." He took up a wide-legged stance and put his hand on his holstered service pistol. "Ms. Leechie, put the crowbar down."

"Oh, thank you, God." Gladys whispered, as she backed out of his way.

"No, Dwayne stole my stuff." She gritted her teeth at the cop. "He stole from all of us. I want my things."

"Linda, don't" Gladys called over. Tadmore gave her a look to silence her. "Sorry, sorry." She winced.

Slowly, the constable drew his weapon, yet pointed it away. He was giving Linda every chance to stand down. "Mrs. Wyatt, please go stand next to the back wall to my left." Tadmore directed her. "You too, Ms. Finkle."

Gladys was more than willing to comply.

Lara followed her, clutching her valuables tight to her chest. "What, what's—"

"Hush," Gladys said, sharply.

They stood together with the concrete wall to their backs. The stack of paper crinkled faintly in Lara's tight grip. With a frown, Gladys saw the certificates had monetary denominations stamped on them.

"Linda," Constable Tadmore said in a calm measured tone. He took a couple steps closer. "It's best to let the RCMP sort out all of this. Then no mistakes will be made, and no one needs to get hurt." He held the pistol with the muzzle pointed down.

The stairway door opened again. This time it was Constable Preeceville. She jogged over, duty belt jingling with the gear she carried.

At first it looked as though Linda was going to argue.

Gladys watched with a worried frown.

Finally, Linda dropped the crowbar and it clattered again to the floor. "Fine, but I'd better get my parent's things back. Lara got her stuff."

Chapter Twenty-Two

"Raise your hands where I can see them." Tadmore ordered.

"Yes, okay," Linda exhaled in frustration and raised her hands.

"Preeceville?" Tadmore asked.

"I got it." Her Smith and Wesson was out of her holster in the same two-handed grip. Index finger beside the trigger guard.

Tadmore holstered his weapon and advanced on Linda. "Please turn around." She did and he grasped her wrists together and snapped on one handcuff. "Can you deal with them?" Following Tadmore's gesture, Preeceville holstered her pistol and crossed over to Gladys and Lara.

"You need to hand over the things you removed from the safe." Preeceville's tone was steely, but Lara never let anyone tell her what to do.

"No. This is my property. That's my safe."

"It's evidence. If you persist, I will charge you with obstructing an officer in the course of performing their duty."

"You wouldn't dare. I'm the victim here." Lara's face was flushed red, probably from anger.

Gladys snorted, trying to contain a harsh laugh. Lara had never been a victim in her whole life.

"I pay your salary. You have no right–"

"Okay, you can just zip it." Preeceville deftly unclipped a set of handcuffs from the back of her belt and snapped one side on Lara's wrist.

"What do you think you're doing?" Lara asked in a shrill voice.

"My job. I only have your word to go by that these items are yours."

"But Linda told you, these are mine." Lara sounded whiny.

"Right, because people who use crowbars to break into other people's homes and storage units are always trustworthy." The constable's tone was sarcastic.

Ah, so the police knew who was responsible for the mess Linda made of the door on unit 103. Gladys was more than a touch relieved.

Preeceville held out her right hand in a 'give it to me' gesture. "You might be involved with Dwayne Davis; we don't know yet. Please hand over the contents of the safe."

"I would never steal." Lara poured outrage into her tone as she clutched the bundle she held in a white-knuckled grip.

"Ha!" Gladys suppressed the rest of her laugh by covering her lips with her left hand and looked away. She had been spending way too much time with Arlie Birch. It appeared she was losing her verbal filter.

Lara rounded on Gladys. "Shut it, you."

"Ms. Finkle." The constable drew Lara's attention away from Gladys.

Jaw jutting out, Lara begrudgingly released the armload of items to Preeceville.

In turn, the cop removed the handcuff from Lara's wrist. "Stay over here by this wall, we don't want anyone to get hurt."

Or touching anything else Gladys surmised. Suddenly she felt drained. This day had been horribly stressful, the last part being the worst. All she wanted was to sit down, put her feet up, and enjoy a cup of strong tea and a cheese bun. She had to settle for leaning on the cold concrete wall.

Preeceville walked into the storage unit and placed the items on top of the safe. Then the cop returned to Tadmore's side and assisted him with Linda who now was becoming defiant. She obviously didn't want the cop to finish handcuffing her.

"Put your hands together, like you're praying." Preeceville instructed her.

"Why are you picking on me?" Linda whined loudly.

"No one is picking on you. You tampered with a crime scene." Sergeant Havelange said. She and Constable Pannu came briskly across the open area from the stairway door.

Pannu took up a position beside Lara and Gladys.

Lara scowled up at the tall, constable, but Gladys was happy to have the officer keeping an eye on them. Thankfully, some of the tension in her shoulders left her and eased the discomfort.

"Hello," she said. "Gladys Wyatt." She held out her right hand.

"Constable Sandro Pannu." He shook her hand.

"Lovely to meet you, Constable."

Lara folded her arms over her chest and gave a derisive sniff.

Preeceville encircled Linda's wrists with two hands.

"No." Linda cried loudly and strained against the hold Preeceville had on her. "Why am I being arrested? I haven't done anything." There was a high note of panic in Linda's voice.

"You aren't being arrested, yet." Tadmore employed a device to the handcuff lock. "You are being detained until we sort this out. So, stay still, that'll allow me to fix the handcuffs from tightening up."

"No, no, no, this can't be happening." Linda's voice was low as she shook her head from side-to-side. Even though a tear trickled down her left cheek, Gladys saw Linda's eyes turn flinty.

The sergeant came to stand in front of her and blocked Gladys' view. "Why are you here, Mrs. Wyatt?"

Before Gladys could answer, the man door, beside the huge garage door, opened. Several heads turned to see who the new arrival was.

Vinny Norquay stuck his head through. "Lara, there you are." He called over. "I've been waiting for you in the parking lot for twenty minutes." Then he gave a start and stumbled through the door.

"Join the others along the wall, please." Another RCMP officer Gladys did not know prodded Vinny inside. He was an inch or so under six feet, dark featured with First Nations ancestry. He kept a firm hand on Vinny's shoulder as he strolled behind the other man. As they got closer, it was easier to see laugh lines were etched around his eyes and an amused twinkle in their dark depths. His name tag read Bighetty.

Bighetty allowed Vinny to walk stiff-legged past the sergeant and over to stand beside Lara, who merely gave him a sour look.

"Thanks for the help, Collin."

"No problem. This looks interesting." He lifted his chin to gesture at the safe." A bit of a mystery?"

Havelange pivoted to look at the large metal box. "Yes, we are only now unraveling it."

Vinny took a slow step backward to lean against the concrete wall. Gladys narrowed her eyes at him. Did Vinny want to be invisible? Why was he here if he had nothing to do with the contents of Lara's safe?

"Hello there, Vinny." Gladys said. "I see you and Lara are friends now. That's better than fighting in the parking lot, isn't it?" She knew her tone was a bit too loud, but she got the sergeant's attention all the same. "Was there any damage to the front of your car after you hit the tree at the end of the driveway?"

The sergeant turned and tipped her head to look between Lara and Vinny. "Fighting? About what?"

Lara waved a hand at Gladys to dismiss he words. "Nothing, we had a slight disagreement, that's all. It's all been rectified."

"So, you paid Vinny the money you owed him, then?" Gladys did not feel like letting the matter go. It was time to get everything out in the open. No more shenanigans.

Constable Bighetty leaned in toward Vinny. "What money was this, then?"

Vinny raised his hands as if to fend off the question. "I did a job for Lara, is all."

Linda lifted her head and frowned at Vinny. "Hey, that's the guy who hooked up my washing machine, and my dishwasher and the hot water heater!" Her voice rose as she spoke. "The floods were all your fault. You sold me bum appliances, and you are a horrible plumber!"

Bighetty gave the sergeant a look. She gave him a nod. "I think you and I should have a quiet chat, Mr. Norquay. Let's go over here." The cop put a hand under Vinny's right arm and persuaded the bald man to accompany him several feet away.

Vinny's eyes darted back to Lara. She turned away from him, ignoring his pleading look.

The sergeant smiled at Lara and then she turned on her heel to enter the storage unit. She did a slow walk around the safe. "What do we have here, Ms. Finkle?" the senior cop asked as she stopped and pulled on one disposable glove.

"The safe is mine. And those papers." Lara lifted her chin and gestured at the metal box situated in the middle of the storage locker. "I think Dwayne thought I kept cash in there and he stole it from me. I reported the theft to that cop, on Monday." She pointed at Tadmore.

"So, you did, I remember reading Constable Tadmore's report." Havelange snapped on the other black disposable glove. "And these certificates." Havelange picked them up and leafed through the pile. "These were removed from the safe, by you? Just now?"

Gladys allowed a slow smile. If she wasn't mistaken, the sergeant was up to something, and she liked where it was going.

"I just said that, didn't I?" Lara was becoming impatient. She shot a quick look at Vinny who was waving his arms as he spoke some distance away, to Constable Bighetty. She frowned when he pointed an index finger directly at her.

"I don't know." The senior cop moved the velvet box aside and sorted through the stack of envelopes and papers. "It might be best if these papers were put back inside, for safe keeping. What do you think, Ms. Finkle?"

Pannu looked away from Lara and rocked back on his heels.

"That would be wonderful." Relief flooded Lara's words. "I'd feel so much better if the bond certificates were back inside the safe."

"I understand." The sergeant straightened and looked over at Lara. "Would you mind opening it then, and put all this back inside please?"

"No, of course not," Lara scurried forward to comply.

Pannu followed, removing his notebook, and stood quietly behind the woman as she knelt down. With the cops looking on, Lara quickly spun the dial, left, right, left, and gave up the combination. The officer recorded the numbers.

Carefully, Lara turned the lever and opened the heavy door. The sergeant first handed Lara the certificates, then followed up with the jewelry box. Lara placed them all neatly and securely back inside the safe.

"Please reengage the locking mechanism." The sergeant directed.

Lara did so and then she stood up. She allowed a small smug smile, relieved to have the thing done as she used her hands to dust dirt off her knees.

The man door opened at the end of the garage. Three white coveralled people filed in. Each were caring equipment cases.

"Sergeant Havelange, you are contaminating my crime scene." The tall one in the front stopped at the storage room door and put his cases on the floor. The other two followed suit, to the left of their leader.

"Couldn't be helped, Williams." She waved at hand at Linda. "We had a break in. Please remove Ms. Leechie, Tadmore."

"This way, ma'am." He led Linda out of the locker and over to the wall.

Next, the sergeant pointed at the metal safe. "This safe contains evidence pertaining to our investigations."

"Oh, handy it's already on a dolly." Williams stuck his hands on his hips as he looked down at the box. "Who has the combination, or do I have to bypass it?"

"I do." Pannu tore a page out of his notebook and handed Williams.

"Lovely." Williams took the paper and also took charge of the unit.

"Wait, that's my safe, and my valuables." Lara surged forward, but Pannu restrained her with one large hand.

"We will catalogue all of it and provide you with a copy, Ms. Finkle." The sergeant strolled over to Lara. "Now, those bearer bonds have serial numbers. Can they be identified as belonging to you?"

"Yes, I have the original purchase receipts stored in my safety deposit box at the bank. I can prove I, or actually my company, owns the bond certificates. The rest of the contents of the safe are assets of Pink Brick too." Lara's haughty attitude was back in full force. "With the exception of the jewelry, it's personally mine and I have it insured."

"Good to know."

Fifty thousand was the denomination Gladys had seen on only one of the certificates. Lara had a whole stack of them at least an inch and a half thick. There was a fortune in that safe. There was only one way Lara could have come into so much money. "Wait a minute." Gladys held up one hand.

The sergeant ignored Gladys and kept on speaking. "We know you own Pink Brick Condominium Properties, Ms. Finkle."

Gladys jerked back her head. "I thought so."

Linda lifted her head and stared at Lara. "You had the building constructed? You are responsible for the crappy plumbing and all this time you let everyone think the flooding was all my fault!"

Lara shrugged dismissively.

The officer in charge held up one hand to forestall Linda's stream of accusations, but it did little. Linda continued to heap abuse on Lara Finkle and her descendants.

His boss gave Tadmore a look that told him to get control of their suspect.

Tadmore turned Linda toward the door. "Let's take a walk, shall we?" He began towing her along.

"That said," Havelange turned back to Lara. "The contents of this safe are considered evidence in our investigations." She said again. "All our investigations." The last words were given a special emphasis. "Even two-year-old investigations."

It took a moment, but Lara finally clued into what she had just done. Lara had laid claim to the safe and everything inside. Her eyes went wide as the cop's meaning, along with the cop's tone, finally seem to penetrate.

Gladys blinked, thinking about what the cop said.

"Did you think we forgot about the missing money your boyfriend, Tim Stanhope made off with?" Her voice carried clearly across the area. "The embezzled funds from the Musgrave Landing village office? There's still a significant amount money unaccounted for."

Linda dug in her feet to prevent Tadmore from moving her. "Ha, probably enough to build a condominium." Her voice echoed back to the rest.

"You can't, you have no right!" Panic made Lara's voice shake. Pannu put a restraining hand on Lara's shoulder when she made a move toward Havelange.

"We have every right." The sergeant pivoted to glance at the safe and then slowly to look back a Lara Finkle. "We will confirm you profited from the proceeds of crime." A forgone conclusion by the sound of it.

Pannu schooled his features as he, too, looked at Lara. "If you cooperate and tell us what was done with all the money, things will go much easier for you."

"I want my lawyer." Lara said and clamped her mouth shut.

"Of course, you do." Havelange nodded.

Gladys caught the satisfied look Pannu shared with Havelange. Arlie had told her the two were the investigating officers for that crime two years ago.

The sergeant said to Pannu. "I think we should make a call to our forensic auditor. I believe her name is Denise McKenzie."

"That's right," he said with a smile. "I bet I have her number right here in my phone. You might want to call Inspector Zeffler, too, he'd want to know too."

"Oh, I plan to call him as soon as we've dealt with all of this." She waved her hand around the general area. "Bighetty, how are we doing?"

Tadmore tried to persuade Linda to move again but she still resisted. "No, I need to hear this." Linda tried to pull away from Tadmore, he was having none of that.

Havelange lifted her chin at Tadmore, and he paused. She gestured with her right hand to wait. He gave her a shallow nod.

Bighetty escorted Vinny back to the group. "This one says he worked for Pink Brick as a plumber for the condo building construction. Then later as a building inspector for this property." He raised black eyebrows at Vinny. "Bit of a conflict of interest wouldn't you say?"

"I bet Lara paid Vinny off to falsify his report to the provincial building authorities." Linda yelled over to the sergeant. "You ruined my life, you creep!" This was shouted at Vinny.

For his part, Vinny stayed tight-lipped and studied the toes of his shiny shoes.

"Couldn't you have kept your mouth shut?" Lara sneered at Vinny. Now he did look up at the owner of Pink Brick.

"Don't worry about it, Lara. I didn't say anything about you and your partner splitting the special assessment fees you charged the unit owners to fix the damages. Nor did I explain about the corners cut fixing the water damage." A slow smile slide across his face.

"Shut up!" Lara snarled.

Pannu reached behind his back and extracted a set of cuffs. "Please turn around." He addressed Lara and she paled. As

Pannu recited the caution statement to her, for once, Lara dropped her head and remained silent.

"Detain Mr. Norquay too, Constable Bighetty. He can give us a statement, at a minimum, and then the Crown can decide what charges should be applied," Havelange said.

"Will do," he said and turned the man around, smoothly removing a set of cuffs at the same time.

Linda had fallen silent as well but instead of looking miserable like Lara did, her eyes narrowed to slits. "I bet Dwayne new about the stolen money. I bet he was blackmailing Lara, just like he was trying to blackmail Freddie. I bet Lara killed Dwayne."

Abruptly, Lara lifted her head and glared at Linda. "Don't be any more stupid than you are."

"Is that true Ms. Finkle?" Pannu asked as he affixed the handcuffs to her wrists behind her back.

"Of course not." Lara snarled and had to spit out a hank of her own blonde hair. Her violent head movement was messing up her hairdo.

Constable Williams picked up the crowbar after his assistant photographed it. He held it in his gloved hands. "Sergeant, if I may interrupt? You'll want to see this."

She walked over to Williams.

He pointed to the stain Gladys had noticed earlier on the tool.

"Is that what I think it is?" the sergeant held the tool up to the dim over-head light as she examined the red-brown stain.

Helpfully, Preeceville snapped on one of the flood lights she'd been helping setup. The rusty-brown residue on the tool took on a more sinister hue. "I'd say this is likely our murder weapon." Havelange cut her yes to Linda and she pinned Tadmore's suspect with her steely gaze. "Now, you're under arrest." She gestured to Tadmore and then turned back to consult with Williams.

"It's not my crowbar, it belongs to Norm." Linda objected.

Gladys watched as her neighbour was forced to walk several feet away to the parked cars. She shied when they came to a stop some feet away from the group, beside the blue Nissan. The constable turned her, and she tried to pull away from him again. "I don't want to do this."

"You don't have much of a choice, Ms. Leechie," Tadmore said and slipped two fingers into her right hip pocket.

Pannu was speaking on his radio. "We have transport about two minutes away, Sergeant." He called over and she waved an acknowledgement.

"Thank you, Constable." The sergeant carefully handed the tool back to Williams. "We have to get that to the coroner."

"I'll take care of it." Williams nodded.

Tadmore continued to search Linda. He used the trunk of Enid's car to lay out the content of her dress pockets. Tissues, some coins, and the pocket watch she'd shown to Gladys. Tadmore set it on the trunk on top of the tissues.

When she saw her father's watch, Linda began a new rant. "It's mine, the watch was my father's. Dwayne stole it like everything else. He got what he deserved."

Gladys lifted her chin and walked a few steps toward her friend. "Constable, the watch actually does belong to Linda. It was her father's. We believe Dwayne stole it along with everything else. He probably had it on him when..." Her voice trailed off.

Tadmore nodded. "If that's the case, we will include it in with the other evidence. If it's yours, Ms. Leechie, you'll get it back."

This seemed to mollify Linda somewhat. She sagged against the back of the car. "I didn't mean to hit him. I took the crowbar for protection." She looked up at Gladys, glassy-eyed. "He just...Dwayne laughed at me. Told me I was weak and stupid. He wouldn't give me my dad's watch back..." She trailed off and dropped her head. Shielding her face with the loose hair that came out of her ponytail.

The cop put the contents of Linda's pockets in evidence bags and Preeceville took charge of them.

"Mrs. Wyatt?" The sergeant was addressing her.

"Yes, sorry." Gladys waved a vague hand at Linda.

"I understand, she is your friend."

"Yes, she is, even if she's done something horrible." Gladys signed.

"I wanted to tell you we found that box of items you mentioned in Mr. Davis' car trunk. Among them, we found your coin collection, the jewelry you identified as missing, and of course as you mentioned down in the garage, your granddaughter's keyboard."

"Oh." Gladys covered her mouth with her right hand. "It was too much to hope for. I was sure Micky's things were gone. Tears prickled in her eyes. Then another thought occurred. "Did you find a pendant? Linda's missing her mother's pendant," she asked the officer.

Linda lifted her head and stared at Gladys as if dazed. "I should have looked harder in the trunk." She shook her head.

"But I couldn't, I didn't have time, Enid started screaming." Linda kicked the tire of Enid's car.

Chapter Twenty-Three

Things moved a bit faster after that.

Linda still looked angry, but unrepentant as she walked jerkily beside of the cop across the last few feet of the garage.

She had to pass the place where Dwayne was killed and that had the effect of silencing her. She was taken out through the garage man door to await transport.

"Just consider every item stolen property until we know different." Williams directed his team. "We'll book it all as evidence." His two helpers glanced at each other; but said nothing. The forensic Ident people continued marking items which would be dusted for fingerprints.

Gladys again felt an overwhelming need to sit down but leaned against the cold concrete wall instead. Did she really need to be here?

"Grandma? Are you all right?" Maisy had just come down the stairs.

"I'm a bit unsteady, is all, it's been a bit of an odd time." She struggled to stand upright as her granddaughter crossed to her.

"You can take Mrs. Wyatt home, if you like. I'll stop up to get her statement as soon as I have things in hand here."

Sergeant Havelange nodded at Maisy. "Thank you for your help."

"No problem." Maisy said and then turned to put an arm around her grandmother. "Come on, I'll make you a strong cup of tea."

They moved toward the exit. "What did you do?" Gladys was feeling slightly better already, if a bit light-headed.

"You gave me your phone. I looked at your recent calls as soon as I left and saw you'd called 911." They began ascending the steps. "Constable Tadmore was on his way here already, I guess. I flagged him down on the road anyway and told him someone had broken into Dwayne's apartment, and you looked scared. I told him it might be Linda."

"I wasn't sure you'd noticed the door to 103 was open."

"I did but see the door was opened. I didn't connect the dots right away even though the whole village had been taking about Mr. Davis' death at the café all afternoon. Sorry about that. It took seeing who you called to do that. I'm sorry I was such a slow dolt."

They entered Gladys' apartment. "You are not a slow dolt. I wouldn't have believed Linda could do something like that if I hadn't seen it with my own eyes." Everything in her apartment was as she'd left it a mere short time ago. Including Albert curled up in his basket, and Blofeld in his customary position high up on his cat post. She breathed out, allowing the past hour's stress to fall away.

"That must have been freaky."

"It was." Gladys collapsed in her armchair in the living room with a sigh.

"Here." Maisy handed over Gladys' phone and then went into the kitchen. "You might want to give Arlie a call. He's been texting and calling constantly." She began filling the kettle. "I think he's worried about you."

"I'll...call him later. After this is all done." She put the phone face down on the side table. It was good just to sit for a bit.

Gladys was half-way through her cup of tea when the sergeant, flanked by Tadmore and Pannu, arrived at her door.

Albert jumped up from his basket and ran around sniffing and demanding attention.

Maisy let them in and offered them tea as well.

"No, but thank you. Mrs. Wyatt, can we get your statement please?"

"Yes, of course." Gladys straightened her spine as she sat up in the armchair. "Have a seat."

Havelange and Pannu sat on the couch across from Gladys while Tadmore hung back in the kitchen. Maisy gave him a shy smile. Tadmore gave her a nod then returned his gaze to his boss, although the tips of his ears turned an interesting shade of red.

Albert decided he needed to sit next to the sergeant's boots.

Pannu got out his occurrence note pad and clicked open a pen.

"Take us back to when you left us in the basement to return home."

Gladys took a breath and recounted the events up until the sergeant appeared back on the scene. "Here's the weird bit." She cleared her throat. "Linda said she used to help her dad install garage doors. That was his business when she was a teenager. That's how he was killed. A door fell on him."

The sergeant nodded in understanding. "Yes, that fits in with everything else."

"And the crowbar." Gladys fidgeted with her tea mug. "You saw the blood stain on the crowbar?"

"We did. It's probably more stolen property. We think from Davis' trunk."

"The crowbar is stolen, but unlike where you found Maisy's keyboard, the crowbar wasn't taken by Dwayne. Linda told Constable Tadmore the tool belongs to Norm Gorlitz, our gardener. She probably stole it from his shed out back." Gladys glanced over at her granddaughter. Maisy's eyes were wide as she listened.

"Constable Tadmore?" Pannu asked making a note.

"Ms. Leechie did say that to me." The young man agreed. "I'll check with Norm Gorlitz." Tadmore left.

The sergeant nodded. "Anything else to add, Mrs. Wyatt?"

"I think it was when Dwayne taunted her with her father's watch that pushed Linda over the edge. He got to her."

The cop frowned. "When was this?"

"At our condo board meeting yesterday. She told me when she was trying to get the condo door open."

"Did you go into the apartment? Did you touch anything?" Pannu asked.

Gladys shook her head. "No, I was just trying to keep her busy until you arrived." Gladys said but waved a hand to brush those thoughts aside. "Never mind that right now. Enid has emergency keys to every apartment in her condo. I don't trust her. What can we do about it?"

"That's how Dwayne did it?" Maisy piped up "He must have taken the keys from Enid's lock box in her utility." The girl shook her head. "The scumbag."

The sergeant compressed her lips, and a sparkle of mirth entered her eyes at Maisy vehemence. "It might be more to it than that. We will have to see."

There was a knock on the door. Maisy hurried across to open it.

"Hey there, Maisy, is Gladys here?" It was Arlie Birch. He strode into the foyer and stopped when he took in the cops. Pale and grim faced he shifted his gaze to Gladys. "Are you all right?"

"Oh my, yes." Gladys got slowly to her feet.

The police did the same. Pannu was called to answer his radio.

"I'm fine now." Gladys' voice only wobbled a bit.

"What's, uh, going on?" Arlie stepped farther into the room and peered into her eyes.

"Too much for a brief explanation." Gladys gave a weak laugh. She used the fingers of her left hand to rub her forehead. The beginnings of a headache was making itself known.

"Sergeant," Pannu addressed his supervisor. "The fingerprints on the safe have been identified."

"Enid Lindquist?"

"The same."

The sergeant nodded and she turned to Gladys. "Thank you, we'll be in touch. There may be more questions after this next arrest."

Gladys blinked as the officers filed past Arlie and crossed the hall to Enid's unit.

Unashamedly, Gladys, Arlie, and Maisy watched from her condo's doorway.

Pannu knocked and after a moment, Enid came to her door.

In short order, Enid was handcuffed, cautioned, and led away. The woman had hardly any time to say anything. It was her sister who fluttered around and demanded to know what was going on and then rushed to the parking lot to follow the cops, with Enid in custody.

"What the heck is going on around here?" Arlie demanded flinging up his hands. His frustration level had reached its peak.

"I don't think the cops needed you to explain the keys in Enid's apartment." Maisy said.

"You're right." Her grandmother said. Then Gladys looked at her friend. "It's been a long event-filled afternoon. Come on, let's get something to eat and I'll bring you up to speed on the craziness."

Chapter Twenty-Four

Maisy sported a goofy smile on her face as she walked up the dock to meet her grandmother.

Gladys could not help but smile too. "Nice young fellow, isn't he? Did he sign your book?"

"He did." Maisy held up the urban fantasy novel with a cover showing a stylized wolf emblazoned on a stone. "He played Iain Trennor in the movie. He was awesome."

"I haven't seen it."

"You should, I'll rent it for us tonight. I think you'll like it."

Gladys' lips twitched. She wasn't sure she would like to see people turning into wolves. She did like Travers in that alternative reality movie where he played an assassin, so who knew. Best to keep an open mind.

The girl let out a little sigh, and then seemed to come back to herself. "Mostly, he wanted to know what all the excitement was up the hill at your place yesterday. So, I brought him up to speed." Maisy offered her grandmother an envelope. "He paid his tab too."

"Thanks." Gladys tucked the money into her vest pocket and picked up the bread racks.

Maisy tucked the paperback into her back pocket. "Grandma, you're making me look bad." She took the racks and led the way back to the station wagon.

After everything was stowed, they climbed in.

"Want a ride to work? Jane wants to talk to me about something. Probably the dinner we are working tomorrow night."

"Yes, please." Maisy clipped on her seat belt.

Five minutes later Gladys parked the big car on the street across from Jane's Eats and Treats. She didn't feel comfortable trying to wedge the station wagon into one of the handful of slots left open in the tiny parking lot. Better to walk a few extra steps.

Maisy held the glass-paneled red door open as the overhead bell tinkled and let her grandmother precede her.

"Hello there," Arlie was wiping down an empty table. He wore the navy golf shirt she'd given him for Christmas last year. It made his eyes look darker blue. He was clean shaven, and his black apron covered his shirt and khaki trousers.

"Hi Arlie. I'll take this to the kitchen." Maisy picked up the grey tub the café used to bus tables.

"Thanks, Maisy."

"Hi Arlie," Gladys said with a smile. "Is Jane around?"

"Yep, in the office." He gestured to the old storage room door. "I'll bring you in a cup of tea, or coffee, shall I?"

"Coffee, yes, please, I'm gasping." She said with a smile and crossed to Jane's office door.

Gladys rapped twice on the closed door and heard the muffled greeting. She opened the portal and walked in.

"Hey there, Gladys, grab a chair." Jane Birch closed the laptop she'd been working on.

"Thank you." Gladys sat and looked up at Jane. "What did you want to talk about?"

Before Jane could say what she wanted, Arlie was there. He offered Gladys a wide-mouthed dark green cup brimming with cappuccino. There was a heart floating in milk froth in the centre of the cup. She took the mug, turned, and smiled up at him.

He careful put another cup down within Jane's reach and strode out the door, closing it behind him.

The two women shared an amused look.

"He's up to something." Gladys lifted her cup from its saucer and took a sip of the hot aromatic liquid.

"I hope not. This has nothing to do with his late-night antics." Jane reached for her own cup.

Gladys swallowed hard and shifted wide eyes to Jane. "You know."

"I do, but it's no big deal. However, he has to stop."

"Uh huh." Gladys said, neutrally.

Jane waved her response aside. "That's not what I wanted to talk to you about. Although my father-in-law knows what we are going to talk about, and he is hoping you'll agree." Jane's words sounded serious.

"Oh?" Gladys blinked and sat a bit straighter in the old wooden office chair. It was tiger oak, like Jane's desk and chair, relics from the past and had belonged to Jane's Aunt Ethel, the former café owner.

"I have a business proposal for you."

"You do?" Was Jane upping her weekly order? That would seriously help. With the arrests of Lara, Linda, Enid, and Vinny, things were about to change with her condo building. What would happen with the strata expenses with four units empty. Only Matthew and Freddie were left beside herself. Freddie was out on bail and would not see a court date for a couple of months yet. If he did time too, what would happen to the building? With Vinny exposed, it was merely a matter of time before the province sent in a real building inspector. Who knew what that one would find?

"Go on."

"I'd like to incorporate your bread baking business into Jane's Eats and Treats. I want the place to truly be a bakery-café. You could use our storefront to sell your products. Or the products could be ours, if you agree to one of the two alternatives I've outlined." She opened a folder and took out two separate sheaves of stapled papers. "These are the two different alternatives. Or, if you'd like to propose a third idea, I'm open to listening to that as well." Gladys quickly read the papers and then looked up at Jane. If she took one of Jane's offers, it would put an end to baking every single day. Her customers would have a set place to buy her product. No more wondering if her product would sell so she would have enough money at the end of the month to pay her mortgage and the strata fees.

She frowned. "I'd still want to keep some of my out-of-town customers."

"Of course, that's no problem, in addition we can add some of my products to yours and give those customers more variety."

"I know several who would appreciate that idea."

"Good." Jane smiled. "Take the papers home with you and re-read them. Talk it over with your financial advisor, there's no rush. Lots of time to think everything over and discuss it with me again when you're ready."

"I'll do that, I'd like to discuss it with my son too."

"Of course." Jane smile turned uncertain. "But you are interested?"

"Heavens, yes, I am very interested." Gladys said with a laugh.

For a moment Gladys envisioned creating her bread and rolls in the huge, well-appointed kitchen. The fragrance of fresh bread filling the café while the sound of cars and trucks rolling forward to embark the waiting ferry.

It was easy to picture herself removing baked loaves and putting the next pans waiting into the commercial stainless-steel ovens. She could double the size of her output.

She could help Arlie, Jane, and Maisy wait on customers. She would be busy but shoulder less responsibility and work with a team.

Gladys lifted her gaze to meet Jane's with a wide smile.

"THREE MURDERS IN TWO years, geez, is there something in the water here?" Arlie opened the metal extension ladder and placed it in its usual spot against the pump house.

"Yes, but the Highmere thing, was that actually a murder?" Gladys paused and leaned on the ladder as Arlie climbed it.

"There was a missing person." She shook her head. "I don't think so, that's not what was in the paper. It couldn't have been a murder."

"Yeah, so they say," Arlie said derisively. He pursed his lips as she handed him the zip ties. "I bet there's more to it."

"Why would the authorities or the Highmeres lie? Get over you conspiracy theory self, please." She handed him the end of the new banner. This time the advertisement offered free ski lessons.

"Humph," he grunted. "Hand me a new zip tie this one is broken on the end."

Gladys tossed another one up and Arlie caught it. "You heard about the partnership Enid had with Dwayne? She'd let him use the emergency keys to get into our apartments. Enid told the police Dwayne was responsible for throwing Albert from the balcony after Albert bit him."

"Yeah, shows Albert is a good judge of character." He pulled the tie tight. "How did Enid get the building manager job with her morals?"

"Lara hired her. She's cut from the same cloth. Lara used the embezzled money from the village to finance Pink Brick and build the condo building. According to Vinny, Lara and Enid were skimming the special assessment funds that were supposed to be used for building repairs."

"Think that's true?"

"Matthew thinks so. He's got a lawyer involved. We may sue to get the funds back. Either way, Lara has money she shouldn't."

"Didn't I say that? I told you Lara still had some of Stanhope's stolen money squirreled away." Arlie's tone was vindicated.

"Yes, you're very smart, now be quiet so I can tell you the rest. Lara bought off Vinny Norquay to get an approved building inspection. He's responsible for all damages from the flooding. There also a link to some other shenanigans Dwayne was involved with like hiring workers for the work crews and getting a kick back."

Arlie paused and looked down at her. "How did you find out that?"

"Constable Tadmore, he stopped by to bring me Micky's ring and coins. Oh, and Maisy's keyboard. He said there was going to be full press release tomorrow, too. I guess the RCMP auditor found a big pile of money Lara still had which they can trace back to the original embezzlement."

"Maybe some of it can go to pay for this silly building."

"One can hope." Gladys gave a nod. "And repair my building."

"What's going to happen with the condo building now? You aren't homeless, are you?"

Gladys narrowed her eyes at Arlie. He looked away and climbed the ladder. "Don't sound so hopeful. I'm not moving in with you."

"I guy can try, can't he."

Gladys smiled and shook her head. She offered Arlie the paper.

"I know you will be okay." Arlie took the other end of the banner and attached it to the drainpipe.

"Anyway," Gladys continued. "Vinny Norquay is going to jail for faking his inspection report. Matthew hopes to get a line on our missing builder through Vinny. Cozying up to Lara was bad for him in the long run."

"Yeah, that backfired. I heard one suggestion of jail time and he gave Lara up just like that." Arlie snapped his fingers. "If the building goes up for sale, it will be a legal mess to unload."

She hadn't planned on telling Arlie about her conversation with her neighbour, but she trusted him. "Matthew doesn't think we have to go that far. I think he might try to buy the rest of the condos. Lara needs to finance her legal team, and so does Enid. Probably Linda too."

"He should be able to pick them up cheap."

"Maybe, I don't know."

"Matthew could flip them," Arlie mused. "Make a decent profit."

"It's possible."

"Linda's going away for a long time." He adjusted the hang of the paper. It was overcast tonight, no moon to make it glow.

"True." Thinking about the events made Gladys sad she'd lost a friend. "I still find it hard to believe Linda killed Dwayne and then had the presence of mind to cover up the murder by diddling the garage door. She never seemed the type. Shows you what I know about people." Gladys shrugged.

"Linda should have just used that crowbar to look in his trunk for her valuables. Dwayne wasn't worth the crack on the head. Or the murder charge."

"Knowing Dwayne, he probably said horrible things to her. He had a way of getting under Linda's skin." Gladys shook her head and held the ladder as Arlie climbed down. Dwayne's unit was repossessed. I'm acting as building manager since Enid is still under arrest. The bank is no doubt going sell the condo off at some point."

Arlie stopped in front of Gladys. "Are you selling your condo?"

At Arlie's careful tone she met his worried eyes.

"I don't think so." Gladys was rewarded with a look a relief from her friend. She knew Arlie wanted to be more than friends, but she wasn't ready for that. At least not yet.

"And why is that?" He climbed down the ladder and gave her his most charming smile. "Don't tell me it's because of Jane's offer."

"Oh, no. It's something else entirely."

"It is?"

"Yes, how do you feel about murder mystery weekends?" Gladys winked at him.

"I have a bad feeling about this." Arlie groused.

The End

If you enjoyed this book, please leave a review.

Don't miss out!

Visit the website below and you can sign up to receive emails whenever Yvonne Rediger publishes a new book. There's no charge and no obligation.

https://books2read.com/r/B-A-SFCV-PODMF

BOOKS 2 READ

Connecting independent readers to independent writers.

Did you love *Condo Crazy*? Then you should read *Death and Cupcakes*[1] by Yvonne Rediger!

[2]

Welcome to Musgrave Landing. A village skirting the Samsum Narrows on Salt Spring Island in the pacific northwest. The quickest way to travel there is to take the ferry from Vancouver Island. You'll arrive right next to Jane's Eats & Treats cafe.

Jane Westcott has come home to Musgrave Landing and nothing will be the same again. She has inherited her aunt's cafe, and a good thing too. Her finances are in a shambles. Her sister receives a letter from their deceased aunt, alluding to finding a key. But where is Jane's letter?

---

1. https://books2read.com/u/49qZ78

2. https://books2read.com/u/49qZ78

The villagers learn the mayor is missing and Jack Birch finds him, murdered. Why is Jane's letter in his coat? Worse, as the investigation unfolds, Jack finds the murder weapon. Turns out it is Jane's gun...

Read more at blackyvy50.wix.com/yvonnerediger.

Also by Yvonne Rediger

Adam Norcross Mysteries
The Wrong Words

Musgrave Landing Mysteries
Death and Cupcakes
Fun With Funerals
Condo Crazy

VIC Shapeshifters
Into the Wood
The Shape of Us
Hell Cat
Trusting the Wolf

Standalone
The Common Touch

Diving In Heart First

Watch for more at blackyvy50.wix.com/yvonnerediger.